BETH

Wilder West Book Three

KAY P. DAWSON

Beth

Print Edition

© Copyright 2021 (As Revised) Kay P. Dawson

CKN Christian Publishing
An Imprint of Wolfpack Publishing
5130 S. Fort Apache Rd. 215-380
Las Vegas, NV 89148

christiankindlenews.com

eBook ISBN: 978-1-63977-063-2
Paperback ISBN: 978-1-63977-064-9

BETH

CHAPTER 1

"**G**et your hands off me right now, or I'll make you regret it!"

The sound of her mother's voice echoed through the walls, into the kitchen where Beth was bending to put a roast of beef into the oven for the hotel dining room supper. Beth slammed the oven door, looking toward Emma, the other woman helping in the kitchen. Their eyes met as they turned to run out to the dining area.

"Why are you resisting, Caroline? Your husband isn't here right now. I saw him heading toward High Ridge earlier today. You know it's still in your blood. Once a whore, always a whore!" Stewart Barlow was a hated man around Mulder Creek, but he didn't care. He thought he owned the town because of the money he had, and he didn't seem to think he had to play by the same rules as others. "I'll pay you good money."

Beth and Emma could hear a struggle, just before they heard the sound of a hand sharply cutting across a cheek.

"There isn't enough money in the world to ever make me want to lie with you, Stewart Barlow, so you can take your filthy hands off me, and get your sorry tail out of my hotel." Caroline's voice shook with anger, but Beth could hear the hurt still under the surface of her mother's voice at the words she knew had stung.

"You stupid woman! How dare you attack me! I'll make you pay for this I promise you. I'll make sure this hotel and restaurant are shut down, and that no one steps foot inside these doors. You should know better than to cross Stewart Barlow. You and your family come into town like you're better than anyone else. But you can't get away from your past, and I assure you, everything you all think you are hiding from people will be common knowledge around here."

By now, Beth and Emma were standing at the doorway and they could see the fury in his eyes. His face was the color of the sun, and his eyes were bulging from their sockets as he yelled in

Caroline's face. He gritted his teeth together, lowering his voice, "You should've just done as I said, and you would have been well paid. Now, this fancy hotel you think you can manage will be nothing but a dream you had as you run back to Chicago with your husband in tow. I'll make sure you pay for your actions today. No one will support a hotel run by a two-bit whore."

Beth couldn't control her fury anymore. Walking straight toward Stewart, she pulled her arm back, balled her hand into a fist, and let him have it directly on his nose. Instantly, blood started to stream down his face, his eyes bulging out even further as he grabbed his hankie to hold to his nose.

She hadn't noticed Sheriff Dixon come in during the commotion, but as she turned, she saw him standing at the door, with his mouth hanging open. She stared him right in the eye as she rubbed her hand, trying not to let on how much it'd hurt.

"Sheriff! Arrest this woman! You saw her attack me. She broke my nose!" Stewart was yelling, causing the blood pouring from his nose to flow even faster. The front of his jacket was covered in red, as he desperately tried to stop the bleeding, while dabbing at the stains.

Nate Dixon still stood staring at Beth. She couldn't tell if he was angry, stunned or something else. He hadn't moved a muscle. Slowly, a smile started to turn up the corners of his mouth, but she noticed he stopped it as quickly as it had started, causing her to wonder if she'd imagined it.

"I assure you, Sheriff, I was only protecting my mother, who was being abused by this man. He had it coming." She lifted her chin a little as she added the last bit.

Finally moving from the doorway, the sheriff walked over toward Stewart. He got up close to his face, looked intently at his nose as Stewart removed the hankie to let him see the damage.

"Nothing looks broken to me. For all I know, you could've tripped and fallen, resulting in your bloody nose." As Stewart huffed, trying to express how absurd he thought that was, the sheriff turned to Caroline.

"Ma'am, was this man bothering you?"

Caroline was visibly shaken. "Yes, sir, he was. He tried to accost me and when I asked him to leave, he threatened me."

"What? You stupid hag!" The sheriff turned abruptly to face Stewart, giving him a look of warning. "You know you were throwing yerself at me, and when I reciprocated the affection, you turned on me!"

"That's enough. Get yourself out of this hotel immediately, Barlow, or you'll be sorry." The sheriff was standing directly in front of him, not letting him get close to Caroline.

Stewart looked at Beth. He walked toward her, growling low under his breath, then spat at her. "You'll be sorry, young lady." The sheriff grabbed him by the arm, throwing him out the door.

Rushing over to her mother, Beth reached for her. "Momma! Are you all right?" She held her mother's shoulders as she looked in her eyes.

Her mother smiled at her. "Yes, Beth, I'm fine. I have handled far worse than him." She walked over and sat down in a chair. "But, Beth, you know it wasn't very ladylike to be hitting a man like that! He could've hurt you!" Beth realized her mother was more shook up over her actions than she was over anything Stewart had said to her.

Casting a glance toward the sheriff to see if he'd heard, she found him watching them intently.

"Beth, you don't need to try hiding anything from me. I was already inside the door when I saw you knock him a good one between the eyes." Nate Dixon was definitely smiling now.

Now feeling embarrassed at how she'd acted, she turned to walk back to the kitchen. "Well, he had it coming." Before leaving the room, she turned to face the sheriff. "And besides, if you saw me hit him, why didn't you arrest me?"

He was fighting hard not to laugh out loud, she could tell, and it just made her angrier. Here she'd come in to protect her mother, and now she was scolded for helping her. And the sheriff seemed to find it amusing that a woman would hit a man like that. She wasn't sure why she'd even come in the room in the first place. Obviously, her help wasn't appreciated.

"I didn't arrest you because I figured he had it coming. I just never expected to see a small slip of a woman be the one to do it." He was grinning from ear to ear, and she noticed the scar that ran across his cheek was more visible when he smiled.

"Yes, Beth, you need to remember that you're a lady, and women just can't go running around hitting men whenever they feel like it!" Her mother was standing back up, walking toward her.

"I didn't exactly hit him just for fun! You heard what he was calling you, Momma! I wasn't going to just sit here and let him talk to you like that." She was hurt that her momma didn't appreciate her help and was now even pointing out to everyone how unladylike she was. As if she didn't already know that.

Beth's friend Emma came to her rescue. "Well, when we heard him trying to attack you, we couldn't just leave you to fend him off on your own! And, if Beth hadn't have done it, I would have." Emma stood tall beside Beth.

She smiled at her friend. Emma had come to Mulder Creek just a short while ago, and they'd become instant friends. When Beth came to help her mother at the hotel, Emma was already working there. She'd faced her own battles and was now engaged to be married to Beth's stepbrother Andrew.

Caroline rolled her eyes at the two younger women standing before her. Knowing she wasn't going to win the argument, she turned to the sheriff. "Can I get you something to eat or drink? I can't thank you enough for helping to get Stewart out of here for us." She looked worried as she continued. "Do you suppose he'll make good on his threats?"

"No, ma'am, I am fine. I only came over because I saw his horse hitched out front and I figured he was likely in here causing some kind of trouble, since that seems to be what he does best." He looked toward Beth who was still standing there listening. "I'd reckon he won't be happy though at having his nose broke by a woman." He was still smirking.

Raising an eyebrow, Beth casually mentioned, "I thought you told him it wasn't broken."

He just shrugged his shoulders. "Oh, I'm pretty sure it's broke, but then again I'm no doc so wasn't really my place to tell him one way or another."

Beth squinted her eyes as she watched him turn back to talk to her mother. For some reason, Nate Dixon hated Stewart Barlow almost as much as she did. It seemed that whenever there was some kind of problem with either Stewart or his son Hank, the sheriff never sided with them. He never allowed anyone to be arrested or charged if they did something to the Barlows.

It was as though he had his own personal vendetta against the men.

For instance, just a few months ago, the time when Beth had come to Mulder Creek with her sister Sarah who'd answered an ad for a mail order bride. It turned out to be Hank Barlow, and luckily for her sister, she'd been saved from ending up with him.

At the time, when they got off the train, and the Barlows were there waiting, there'd also been another man who they knew. After a huge confrontation, Sarah had ended up married to the other man, Jake Montgomery. And, as Beth thought back about it, she realized, Sheriff Dixon had been a huge factor in making sure the Barlows didn't get their hands on Sarah by suggesting Jake marry her instead.

The more she thought about it, she could remember other times when the sheriff had stepped in, at a cost to the Barlow men. She wondered what the story behind it all was.

She listened as her mother told the sheriff exactly what had happened today in the hotel. When she heard her mother get to the part about Stewart putting his hands on her, and calling her a whore, she was seeing red again.

Her mother had been through so much, and now she finally had this hotel that was all hers. She was now married to Alistair McConnell, who loved her deeply and who accepted her for who she was. That hadn't always been the case for Caroline.

After her parents had died when she was a

young girl, she'd been taken in by a woman who happened to own a brothel in Chicago. Eventually, to support herself, Caroline had been pulled into that life. Luckily for her though, a man named Thomas Elliott had come in on her first night, falling head over heels for her.

But he was also a society man and was to be married to a woman who'd bring the wealth that they needed back to the family. He'd never been able to stand up to his family and acknowledge the woman he loved, ending up married to the other woman.

He eventually set up an apartment for Caroline, where he would spend many years coming in and out of their lives as Caroline raised the three daughters they'd have together.

It wasn't a life she was proud of, but Beth was fiercely protective of her mother. She'd always held her head up high and shown her daughters to be proud of who they were. They'd never been given their father's name, going instead with their mother's last name, Wilder. It was a name she was greatly proud of.

Beth would do anything for her. Even if it meant hitting some man square on the nose who dared to call her a whore.

CHAPTER 2

Nate walked across the street toward his office. He kept replaying in his mind the moment that he walked in the door of the hotel and saw Beth punching Stewart Barlow.

He'd heard the comment the man made to Caroline and was about to intervene when he saw Beth walk over as though she were merely going over to say hello. He'd watched her face and saw the exact moment she rolled her fingers into fists. Before he had a chance to stop her, she already had blood pouring from the man's nose.

He shook his head as he chuckled low in his throat. He knew it wasn't funny, because Stewart Barlow wasn't a man to be messed with, and he already hated the entire Wilder family. This latest incident was only going to cause more trouble for them.

But to have witnessed the man being taken out by a woman who barely came up to his chest, was truly something to remember

As he was going in the door, he heard Beth's voice as she ran up behind him. "Sheriff Dixon, wait!"

He turned, leaning against the doorframe as he watched the stunning woman run across the street toward him. He'd have to be blind not to notice how beautiful she was. "I've told you a hundred times, you can call me Nate. I'd think I've known you and your family long enough now to do away with the formal names."

"Sorry, you're right. Nate. Anyway, can I talk to you for a minute? I have to get back and help Momma fix supper for the hotel, but I managed to sneak away so I could talk to you." She flashed her dazzling smile in his direction, but he wasn't fooled. He knew with Beth she was more than likely up to something that he didn't know if he wanted to get dragged into.

He raised his eyebrow at her. "I suppose I could spare a couple minutes." Moving to the side, he let her go in the door ahead of him.

He followed her in, hanging his hat on the

hook inside the door, then headed over to sit down by his desk. Leaning back in his chair, he put his feet up on the table and crossed his arms over his chest while he waited to see what Beth wanted.

"I actually have a couple things I need to talk to you about. I heard you mention to Momma the other day when you were in having lunch that you needed someone to help you around here to keep up with papers and other jobs. I know you're really busy having to be sheriff for the whole area between Mulder Creek and High Ridge, so I hoped maybe I could help you out."

She was trying not to let on that she was nervous. He'd noticed with Beth when she was feeling anxious about something, she'd twirl her hair that was always falling out around her pins.

"And why would you want to work here? You have a perfectly good job at the hotel with your mom."

"Yes, I know, and I'd still help her out over there. But I need to feel like I am doing something for myself too." She walked over and looked out the window. "I hate feeling like I am just a burden. Momma has Emma working at the hotel, and I know I help too. But I just feel the need to do something that is for me."

She turned back around, pinning him to the spot with those violet eyes. "I'm almost past marrying age, and I need to secure my own future." She scowled at him when he laughed out loud.

"You're hardly an old spinster! I'm pretty sure you still have many years left to find yourself a husband. What is this really about?"

Finally deciding to just tell him the truth, she blurted out, "I want to find dirt on Stewart Barlow so he'll leave us alone." She stood waiting to see his reaction.

"Nate, I know there's something between you and the Barlows. You hate them as much as I do; it's obvious whenever you're around them. I thought if you and I worked together, we could find some way to make them pay for everything they keep getting away with around here. I'm tired of them always trying to hurt people I care about."

Nate still sat staring at her. This woman had managed to leave him at a complete loss for words twice in the same day. He didn't know how to react. The woman standing in front of him was no wilting flower, that was obvious.

"Well, how do you figure working here, helping me around the office, will get you any closer to finding out "dirt", as you put it, on Barlow?" He dropped his feet to the ground, leaning forward and crossing his arms on the table in front of him. "Don't you think if I had something, I'd have done something about it by now?"

"I just thought that with the two of us putting our heads together, we could figure something out. Or catch him doing something he shouldn't be." Trying to give him even more reasons, she added, "Besides, I need my own money. My trust fund from my father's death won't be available to me until I am twenty-one. I don't want Momma paying me for helping her. I just need to be doing something more than waiting around for a man to come along and sweep me off my feet!"

All Nate could do was sit and shake his head. Beth was not the kind of woman he was used to seeing. Most women would love to just sit around and wait for a man to come along and take care of them. Not Beth.

And, to make sure she wasn't at all like any other women, she also wanted to work with a sheriff to try and find a way to catch the town's most dangerous man in some kind of activity that'd make him pay for everything he'd done to so many people.

He just didn't even know what to say, and he normally wasn't a man who got tongue tied easily.

"Are you going to answer me, Nate? Or just sit there looking at me like I have horns growing out of my head?" She was standing with her hands on her hips waiting for him to reply.

"Beth, I just don't need to be worrying about you getting hurt at the hands of the Barlow men. I don't mind you working here to help me with some of the tasks that are tedious, like sorting paperwork and keeping the office clean, but I can't have you running off to try catching them doing something wrong." He didn't need the worry of her getting hurt while he was trying to uphold the law in this area.

"I promise, I won't do that. I'll just work here with you now and then, keeping the office sorted and neat. I'll help you with paperwork and anything else you need doing between the jobs Momma has me doing at the hotel. And, if we can come across some way to catch the Barlows while we're working, then that will just be an added bonus to me being here." She was smiling from ear to ear, and Nate had to stop his heart from fluttering when he looked at her.

He didn't know if having her around would be a good idea, but he figured she'd be safer here than on the street trying to catch Barlow herself. And, he had no doubt with Beth that she would be doing exactly that.

"You never told me what your problem with Stewart Barlow was either. I know there's some reason you hate him as much as you do. You aren't the kind of man who holds a grudge against someone for no reason." She wasn't going to drop the question he'd hoped she'd forgotten she had asked earlier.

Nate hadn't ever told anyone the story behind him and Stewart Barlow. He'd never really felt the need or found anyone he could even trust enough. But, for reasons he couldn't understand, he felt like he could tell Beth.

She sat down in the chair on the other side of the table, putting her elbows onto the table to look directly at him. One thing about Beth Wilder, you could read her like an open book. She was waiting for him to talk, and she wasn't going to leave until he did.

"There isn't much to tell. Stewart Barlow is my step-father."

"What!" Beth jumped out of her chair, slapping her hands onto the table. Her reaction was exactly what he'd thought it would be. Most people would try to control their shock, hiding it inside, but not Beth.

"Beth, will you just sit down. All your jumping up and down is hard on my neck." He turned in his chair a bit so he could put his legs out to full length. He looked out the window as he related the story behind him and Stewart.

"Barlow is my step-father, as I said. Or, should I say, was. My mother died when I was young, while she was still married to the man. I only lived with him for a short while. He'd been friends with my Pa, and when he died during a hunting accident, Stewart comforted my mother. They eventually got married."

He turned to see her reaction, and she was sitting there with her mouth hanging open. Her eyes were larger than his belt buckle, he was sure.

"I never liked him. I missed my Pa terribly, and Stewart never tried to be nice to me. Once he married my mother, he became even meaner."

He put his eyes down to his boots, unsure if he should tell her any more.

"What did he do to you, Nate?" Beth asked so quietly he barely heard. He lifted his head, rubbing his finger down the scar that ran across his cheek and down onto his neck.

"One night he whipped me something awful

over a stupid fight I had with Hank. When my Ma saw what he'd done, she sent me with all my belongings to stay with an aunt who lived in Montana. That was the last I ever saw my Ma."

He stood up, moving to the window unable to see the pain in Beth's eyes. "Every time I see this scar reflected back at me I am reminded of that night. My mother was terrified, and I begged her to come with me. He wouldn't let her. She had to sneak me out, put me on a train with a letter for my aunt. I've never forgiven him."

He hadn't heard Beth walk up behind him. "That's awful, Nate!"

He shook his head free of the memories that were starting to crush him. He turned around and pushed himself away from the window, moving toward the door.

"It's getting late, and you have to help your Ma get the evening meal done for the hotel guests. I'll walk you back over." He wasn't going to tell her any more. He didn't like the feeling of anyone pitying him. He'd learned long ago that feeling sorry wasn't going to change anything.

He'd vowed all those years ago he would come back, and he'd make Stewart Barlow pay somehow. But he wasn't going to stoop to his level. That's why he became a lawman, determined to make him face his dues. He'd come back to Mulder Creek to keep an eye on Barlow, waiting for him to slip up.

He had a score to settle with that man. Because what he hadn't told Beth, and what he'd never told another living soul, was that he had no doubt in his mind Stewart Barlow had killed his Ma.

And he was here to prove it.

CHAPTER 3

Beth ran the words Nate had spoken yesterday over and over in her head. She had no idea Stewart Barlow was his step-father! And she could understand now his hatred for the man. He'd left a scar for Nate to always remember what had happened, and she knew how self-conscious he was about it, even if he didn't realize it himself.

Any time a woman would come near him, he always turned that side of his face away. Not all the way, just enough so the scar wouldn't be obvious. But as she'd got to know him over the past few months, he'd let his guard slip when he was around her sometimes, and she'd seen the way the scar tore across his cheek, pulling the skin tight where it continued down his neck.

As she thought about the little boy suffering at the hands of that man, she didn't even realize she was crumpling the paper up as violently as she was until she heard Nate across the room. "Whoa there! You can just throw the paper into the basket by the door. You don't need to beat it to death first."

She lifted her head to look over at him. He was looking at some papers he had for the judge who was coming through town today.

"Sorry, I was thinking of something else and I guess I got a little carried away." She offered him a weak smile and noticed him raise an eyebrow at her in question. Putting her eyes back down to the task she'd been assigned, she went through more of the papers, seeing which ones she could discard and what she had to set to the side.

She hated that man even more now. Not only had he insisted on bothering her mother at every turn, showing up and harassing her, calling her a whore and anything else he could think of, he'd also caused a great deal of anguish for her family. He'd arranged for her sister Sarah to find an ad to come out and marry his son Hank, for no other reason than to get back at a man he hated.

There were also rumors that he was behind the cattle rustling incident that had caused her sister Sarah's husband to get shot. Thankfully, Jake wasn't killed, but Stewart had made it clear he wasn't to be trifled with. Of course, like always, it'd never been proven. However, Beth was sure Nate was still working on finding any evidence he could to point in that direction.

Now, to find out what he'd done all those years ago to a little boy and his mother, broke her heart. The sooner they could rid the town of that man, the sooner everyone could rest easier.

She snuck a glance over to where Nate was focusing on a piece of paper in front of him. His brows were furrowed as he concentrated, unaware of her watching him. She wasn't sure what it was about him that always drew her to him.

Her eyes focused on the full head of dark wavy hair that always seemed to have a mind of its own when his hat came off. His shoulders were wide, and she could see the muscle in the arms under the rolled up sleeves. She knew he had bright blue eyes, and as she sat looking at him, those same eyes lifted to meet hers.

Feeling her cheeks begin to burn, she quickly put her gaze back down to the papers she was working on.

As she tried to get her mind back on her job, she noticed an envelope sitting at the edge of the desk with Nate's name on it. Seeing it hadn't been opened yet, she stood up to take it over to him.

He looked up from his desk as she walked over. "I found this in that stack of papers, Nate. It looks like a letter to you that you haven't opened yet." She handed it to him.

He took the envelope from her, but just sat and stared at it. If she didn't know him better, she'd almost believe he was blushing a bit.

He quickly tried to tuck it into a drawer. "It's nothing."

She crossed her arms in front of her, giving him a look indicating she didn't believe him. "If it's nothing, why do you look like you just got caught peeking under a woman's dress?" She almost laughed at the expression he gave her. "It was obviously a woman's handwriting, so who was it from Nate?"

He tipped back in his chair, putting his arms across his chest to mimic her own stance. "Not sure why you think it's any business of yours, but if you really feel you must know, it's from a woman I've been writing to back east."

Her mouth gaped as she realized what he meant. "You mean you put in an ad for a bride?" She never thought he'd be the type to do something like that.

"Listen, it gets lonely out here. I saw how well things worked out for Ben when your sister Everly answered his ad, and even though your other sister came out answering an ad for another man, she ended up pretty happy with what she got in the end. I just figured it couldn't hurt to see what was out there." He stood up, coming around the desk to stand beside her. "It isn't like I have the kind of face that draws women to me around here."

She stood rooted to the spot unsure she'd heard him right. "What do you mean? There's nothing wrong with your face." She turned to go back to her work. "It's more likely your attitude that scares women away from you." She never saw the grin that covered his face when he heard that remark.

Sitting back down to her stack of papers, she watched him sit down at his own desk and reach in to take the letter out. She watched him read it, then jumped when he cursed loudly.

"What is it?" She'd dropped some papers on the floor at his outburst, so she bent to pick them up.

"It says she's coming out to meet me! She sent the letter weeks ago, and she is due to come here tomorrow. I don't even know where she will stay or anything. My room in the boarding house really isn't suitable. Why didn't she wait to hear back from me?" He was up now, pacing the room.

"She can stay with us at the hotel, Nate. You should be excited. The woman you'll quite possibly end up falling in love with is on her way to meet you!" Beth wasn't sure why she felt a twinge in her stomach when she said those words to him, but she just brushed it aside.

"Considering we've only wrote one letter to each other, I'm hardly inclined to believe we'll be falling madly in love. I can't imagine why she'd think she needed to rush out here without waiting for me to send her the money for a ticket."

"Maybe she just couldn't wait to meet you. I'm sure she saw your charming personality and just couldn't wait a moment more." Beth was enjoying watching him squirm.

He shot her a look that showed he wasn't in the mood to joke around. "Oh, I'm sure if she gets to spend any time with you, she'll get to hear all about my charming personality."

Smiling sweetly, she replied, "You can bet on it."

THIS WAS NOT what he needed right now.

He'd only put the ad in that magazine on a whim, never really thinking anyone would reply. When he'd received a letter from some woman named Susan in New York, he hadn't even been sure he'd write back. He only did after Beth had moved into the hotel across the street, and after spending some time there, he'd come to realize that women like her would never settle for someone like him. He'd decided to reply and see what she was like.

There weren't many single women around Mulder Creek. Those who were, either had serious personality issues, or they were women like Beth who'd be able to have their pick of any man in the area. He knew he wouldn't be considered a catch for anyone.

He tried not to let the scar that cut across his face bother him, but when he found himself around beautiful women, he couldn't help it. He knew that was always the first thing they'd see. And, the worst part was, he hadn't had the chance to tell Susan to prepare her, and now she was on a train out west to meet him.

He knew what her reaction would be. It was always the same. Most people would try to act like they didn't notice it, but their eyes always gave them away.

Beth was honestly the only woman who never made a fuss about it, and in fact, often made him feel like he was making a big deal out of nothing.

And now he had a woman heading out here to meet him, one he knew nothing about, and he was expected to court her and see if they'd be suitable for marriage. What had he got himself into?

He stood perfectly still on the platform as he heard the whistle from the train in the distance. Suddenly, he could sense someone walking up beside him. Turning his head slightly, he could see Beth rushing up, pulling at her shawl as the wind threatened to rip it from her grasp.

"What are you doing here, Beth?" he sighed.

"Well, I thought I should be here too since she's going to be staying with me at the hotel." She looked like she was genuinely hurt that he'd ask her that. He knew differently though. She was enjoying this mess he had created with the woman headed his way and didn't want to miss any of the drama unfold.

She gave him the biggest smile she could, trying to convince him she was sincerely here to be helpful, but all he could answer was, "Umhmm."

Turning back toward the track, he added, "Are you sure you aren't here to witness how uncomfortable things are about to become for me?" Raising an eyebrow, he glanced over her way.

"Oh, you're being such a downer. Maybe you'll really like this girl, you don't even know. You aren't even giving her a chance. Besides, you're the one who put the ad in the paper, remember? You're the only one you can blame."

Turning to face her, he looked at her incredulously. "Are you serious? I wrote one letter. One letter! I never thought she would take it upon herself to come out here without corresponding for a while to see if we were suited. I know nothing about her. And she knows nothing about me. I can't even imagine why she'd jump on the first train west other than she is seven feet tall, missing all her teeth and has warts on her nose."

He was getting aggravated the more he thought about it, and Beth being here wasn't helping. Although, hearing her laugh out loud at his last comment finally broke the tension he was feeling a bit. He ended up smiling too, even though he was sure he likely wasn't too far off the mark.

"Give her a chance. You never know." Beth was still laughing.

The train came around the bend at the end of town. He felt like his insides were twisted in knots, and as he glanced at Beth, he secretly wished it were her getting off the train to meet him. Shaking his head free of the thoughts, he pulled his hat off his head to get ready to greet the woman who'd come all this way to meet him.

After the smoke cleared and the dust had settled, the doors finally opened. There were a few other travelers getting off the train, meeting up with their loved ones. Just when he thought maybe she'd missed the train, he noticed a woman stepping off, taking the hand of the conductor as he helped her down to the platform.

He was sure his jaw hit the ground, and he heard Beth take in her breath. Surely this wasn't Susan.

The woman stepping off the train was stunning. Her hair was the color of butter, and she was dressed like she'd just come back from her coming out ball in the finest society. She wore white gloves that covered her arms up to her elbows, and her dress had layer upon layer of the most delicate white silk.

He looked at Beth in disbelief, noting she was

staring at the woman in awe. "No warts on her, that's for sure," was all she said, without taking her eyes off the woman.

He walked over to her, deciding to push his hat back on his head to prevent too much of a shock upon seeing his face. He sensed this woman was more delicate than most, and he didn't want to scare her off.

She turned toward him as he got closer, and her eyes were the bluest blue he'd ever seen. The exact opposite of Beth's dark eyes. Again, shaking his head, he silently chastised himself for comparing the woman to Beth already.

"You must be Susan." When she gave her head a graceful nod, he continued, "I'm Nate, the man you've been writing to. And this is Beth. She works at the hotel across the street and has arranged for you to stay there while we have the chance to get to know one another."

The woman set her hand out for him to place a kiss on the top. He'd never been around any woman like this, so he wasn't sure if he was doing it correctly, but he took her hand placing a light kiss on the glove.

"Well, I do hope the hotel is clean. I am positively filthy after sitting on this train. And the dust around here is atrocious! How can you stand it?" She was looking at Beth now, giving her a look up and down indicating how much distaste she had for the attire she was wearing.

"You can take my bags and unpack them for me." She turned her back to Beth, pulling out a parasol and putting it over her head. She'd never even looked at Nate, except for the brief nod of her head.

Nate wasn't sure what had just happened, but he could see Beth was about to breathe fire. "No, that's fine, Susan. I'll carry your bags across to the hotel and we can get you settled in."

Again, the thought of what had he got himself into raced through his mind. The few moments he'd seen her first step off the train had been instantly tainted when she opened her mouth to speak. He truly hoped it was just the exhaustion from the trip making her act like this, because if it wasn't, he wasn't sure he could keep Beth from causing her bodily harm.

And, the worst part was, he wasn't sure if he'd even want to stop her.

CHAPTER 4

Beth sat on a bench just to the side of the makeshift dance floor. Today, her step-brother Andrew had married her friend Emma, and the day had been full of food, laughter and fun. She was thrilled to see them both so happy together, truly in love and ready to spend their lives with each other.

Her mother had set up a beautiful wedding location just behind the hotel. They'd moved all the tables outside and made a dance floor out of pieces of wood given to them from the lumber mill.

She looked out at the dance floor that still had couples moving together. She saw her oldest sister Everly dancing with her husband Ben. Sarah and Jake danced by, as did her newly-married mother and Alistair McConnell. She smiled, realizing just how much her family had come through and changed over the past couple of years.

Everyone had found their happy ever after, with someone they could spend the rest of their lives with.

She tried to swallow the lump that built in her throat. She was happy for everyone, she really was. So why did she feel just a bit of sadness today?

She wasn't the type of woman who needed a man to make her happy. She didn't see herself pining away over love.

But, deep down, she still longed for what she saw her sisters had. She noticed how Ben looked at Everly, and how Jake's eyes seemed to look right into Sarah's soul. She saw the joy they found in each other, and she sometimes found herself wishing she could have the same.

As she sat there, she noticed Nate escorting Susan to a bench across the floor. Susan didn't seem to be having much fun. She sat fanning herself most of the day, and Beth had watched as Nate tried to keep her comfortable, bringing her water to drink and even taking her inside so she could change when she felt her outfit was getting too dirty.

She couldn't figure the woman out. She was horribly spoiled and seemed to hate it here. So, Beth couldn't make out why she even came.

The part that bothered her the most was the way she treated Nate.

Beth had seen how she didn't even look at him when she got off the train the other day. But she'd noticed how he put his hat on and kept the side of his face turned away from her. He was still doing it whenever he was around Susan, and it made Beth's blood boil.

She didn't know why he was so worried about that scar. It wasn't even disfiguring, but she always noticed how he kept his head turned enough to keep it from people's view.

And it seemed like no matter what he did, Susan wasn't happy. She hated the heat, she hated the dust, and the clothes she was wearing were not suited for out west at all. Beth had tried to lend her some of hers to wear, and she thought the woman was going to faint at the suggestion.

Susan was not at all suited for Nate. And, as Beth sat there watching, she noticed him look in her direction. He looked tired, but he gave her a smile. When he did, she felt her heart skip a beat.

Why was he having this effect on her lately?

She knew they'd spent a few days working in his office together, but she didn't think that was it.

Was she jealous?

The thought hit her hard in the stomach. She didn't have feelings for Nate Dixon like that, did she? She thought of him as a friend, and enjoyed being around him, but was there more?

She shook her head, smiling back at him. He shrugged his shoulders, while rolling his eyes toward the woman who was busy fanning herself beside him. Just then, Jake came over sweeping down into a deep bow before her and asked her to dance. Beth jumped up, glad to get her mind off the man across from her. She took Jake's hand, and they moved onto the dance floor.

After their dance, they headed over to the table for a lemonade. Her sister Sarah was standing there, and Jake bent down to kiss her lightly on the cheek. Beth felt her stomach flutter at the love she saw between them.

"Are you getting tired, love?" Sarah had just told them all that she was going to have a baby, and Beth could see that Jake didn't want her overdoing it. Everyone was staying in the hotel tonight as the trip back to High Ridge would be too long.

"I'm fine, Jake. Stop fussing over me." Sarah took his hand. "Come on, let's dance some more!"

Beth smiled as she watched Sarah pull him back onto the dance floor. As she watched, she noticed Susan had agreed to dance with Nate. She saw him take her hand and lead her to the floor. She even thought she saw her smile a bit.

She could feel a hole gnawing at the bottom of her stomach, and she tried to ignore the feeling as she watched the two of them moving together. Nate had his hand on her back, and they were talking to each other, seeming to finally be taking the chance to spend some time together. She guessed after getting to know him, and sitting talking with him today, Susan had realized what a good man Nate was.

Hoping not to let anyone see the pain in her eyes as she watched them, she turned to walk away. She thought she could take a walk in the evening air, and clear the thoughts that'd been working their way in.

Walking away from the hotel, she tried to figure out what was causing her to feel this way. She'd known Nate for weeks, but since Susan had shown up, it was like she was seeing him in a different way. She wasn't sure how to handle the feelings she was having, especially now that there was a woman here who'd come all this way hoping to marry Nate.

It wasn't like she'd just be leaving.

Pulling her shawl up tighter around her shoulders, she decided to head toward the stables. Horses were her first love, and she'd spent many hours working in the stables in Chicago. She missed being around them, and whenever she got the chance, or needed to get away, she found herself drawn to be near the animals.

As she got closer to the stables, she could hear a commotion over by the saloon. Ducking inside with the horses, she peeked her head back out looking toward the noise. She could see Hank and Stewart Barlow arguing with some men, and by the way they were all acting, she was sure they'd all had too much to drink.

Clenching her teeth, she put her head back in and walked over to where a beautiful tan horse was tied up near the back. Picking up a brush she saw sitting on a stool beside it, she started to brush down the neck.

She should've known it would be the Barlows causing the disturbance. She was surprised they hadn't tried to come to the wedding, although the night wasn't over, so she guessed there was still time. In fact, as she thought about it, that would make sense as to why they'd even be in town in the first place.

Sure, they were going to head that way to cause trouble, she turned to go back and let the others know they were in town. She'd been so engrossed in brushing the horse down, she hadn't noticed anyone walk into the stables.

She walked straight into Hank Barlow.

He grabbed her arms, pushing her back against the far wall. The horse she'd been grooming started to paw at the ground, whinnying and pulling at its rope.

"Well lookee here...ain't I in luck today?" He sneered in her face, putting both her wrists in one hand while he grabbed her chin and lifted her face up with the other.

"Let go of me, Hank. The others all know I'm here and will be coming to look for me." She didn't want to let him see the fear that was starting to grip her.

"Oh, I'm pretty sure everyone is having so much fun at the wedding, they ain't gonna miss you for a while." He was starting to hurt her arms, and he had her head pressed back into the wall so she couldn't even turn her face away from him. His breath filled her nose with the smell of whiskey.

Pushing his face down to hers, he tried to kiss her. Instinctively, she brought her knee up, catching him between his legs. He buckled over, letting go of her arms.

She ran to get past him, but he reached his hand out and wrapped his fingers tightly around her arm. He threw her to the ground, climbing on top of her. Covering her mouth with his grimy hand, he hissed in her face. "You shouldn't have done that, you stupid whore! You're no better than your mother, prancing around showing off your skirts, then gettin' mad when a man tries to take notice."

Beth squirmed violently beneath him, trying to shake him off her. She could feel blood on her lip where he was pushing so hard on her mouth. She could feel him trying to undo his belt buckle, and she knew she had to move now while he was focusing on that.

Thrusting her waist up, she felt him go off balance. Just then, she could hear a voice yelling her name, but she couldn't think. Fear, and the need to protect herself, had taken over. When he started to fall to the side, she gave a mighty push, making sure he'd fall clear from her so she could get up and run.

As he fell to the ground, she heard a dull thud

as his head struck something on the ground. She tried getting up, not even noticing the hand that had reached out for her.

"Beth! Listen to me, Beth. It's me, Nate." Finally hearing his voice cut through the racing in her head, she turned to see Nate. Falling into his arms, she sobbed, shaking at the realization she was safe.

"What is going on in here!" Stewart's voice cut through the air as he pushed past them. Bending down to his son, he rolled him to the side, noting the blood that was covering the rock he'd landed hard on. "Hank. Hank! Are you all right?" His voice reached a high pitch as he kept calling his name, not getting any response.

"What have you done? You killed him!" Stewart flew toward Beth, grabbing at her.

Nate pulled her behind him, stopping Stewart in his tracks. "You won't lay one finger on her, Barlow. Your son was attacking her. I saw it with my own eyes when I walked in. All she did was push him off her. He did it to himself." Beth was having a hard time understanding everything they were saying. Hank was dead? She'd killed him?

Stewart was shouting and pushing at Nate, causing enough of a commotion to bring others running. As she saw Sarah and Jake run through the door, and the look on their faces as they saw what had happened, Beth felt like she was going to be sick. Sarah's hands flew to cover her mouth, and Jake ran over to hold Stewart away from Nate, who was desperately trying to keep him away from Beth.

"I want this woman arrested, Dixon! She killed Hank and I want her to pay!" At those words, Beth could feel the world around her start to spin. She couldn't feel her legs anymore, and blackness started to close in around her. She felt strong arms go around her as she heard the sound of Nate's voice saying her name from far away.

Her last thought was that Nate would take care of her as she lost her grip with consciousness.

CHAPTER 5

When Old Pete arrived, the man who ran the stables, Nate ordered him to close the stables up for the night, until he could get back and take care of things.

Nate then carried the woman in his arms across the street toward his office. When he'd walked through those doors and seen Hank on top of her, he thought he was going to kill the man himself. He saw him reaching to undo his belt and noticed the moment Beth bucked up to knock him off, pushing him as he lost his balance.

His heart had felt like it had been ripped from his chest when she finally seemed to hear him through the fog and let herself fall into his arms.

He'd seen the terror in her eyes, and he silently cursed himself for not getting there sooner.

He'd noticed her leave the wedding while he was up dancing with Susan. He'd wanted to go with her, sensing she was upset about something, but he couldn't just leave Susan behind. She'd finally agreed to dance after a day spent complaining, so he'd jumped at the chance to do anything besides sit and listen to her talking about how hot she was, or how dirty she felt.

Jake rushed ahead and opened the door to Nate's office as he carried her in. Sarah was crying as she ran ahead to get the doctor, and to let the others know what had happened, while Stewart was still calling loudly to anyone who would listen for her to be arrested.

Nate couldn't think. All he could see was the face of the woman he held in his arms as he gently laid her on a cot. Needing to take his anger out on someone, he turned to face Stewart.

"Listen to me, old man. You will back off. Your son attacked this woman, and I will not be forced into arresting anyone just because you say so. I'm still the law around here, and I will decide. Do I make myself clear?" His teeth were clenched as he growled the words out, pushing his finger into the man's chest to make sure he understood.

Stewart wasn't backing down. "I don't care if you are the law. You know as well as I do that when someone is killed, the murderer has to be held to go before the judge. You will arrest her, or I'll go and get someone who will." The older Barlow man knew he had Nate backed into a corner. If he went to get a judge or sheriff from a neighboring community, things could go badly for Beth.

Nate needed to keep her here where he could make sure she was safe until the judge could get here.

He could feel his jaw starting to hurt where he was clenching it together so tightly. Just then, the rest of the wedding crowd arrived, with Caroline pushing through the door first. She raced over to her daughter lying on the cot. "What happened, Nate?" She looked to him for an answer. "Sarah said she was attacked."

"What happened, is that your daughter is just like you, taunting the men around these parts with her wares, then taking offense when a man tries to pay her any attention. This time she went too far, and now my son is dead!" Stewart was yelling at Caroline.

Before he could even think, Nate had him by the throat, holding him against the wall by the door. "Get out of my office. I don't want to see your face around here until the judge gets here. Until then, get out of my sight."

"If you arrest her, I'll walk out the door this minute. But not until I know she'll face the judge for what she did to my son." Stewart's face was turning purple, but he wasn't ready to back down yet.

"I will arrest her, just to keep her away from you. But I promise you, she will not pay for a thing that has happened here tonight. I will make sure of it." With that, he pushed Stewart toward the door.

They could hear Beth starting to wake up, as she reached up to rub her head. "What happened? Where am I?" She sat up on the cot, pulling her legs over the side. Noticing everyone standing around, she put her hand to her mouth as she remembered.

"Oh no!" Jumping to her feet, she raced over to him, taking his hands into hers. "Please Nate, tell me I didn't kill Hank!" Tears were starting to fall down her cheeks as she remembered everything.

He put her hands into his and pulled them to his chest. "Beth, Hank attacked you. You didn't kill him. You were only protecting yourself from him. What happened was an accident." He looked into her eyes, wanting to erase the fear and memory of the attack away.

She turned and walked back to the cot, slowly sinking down onto it. She lifted her head to look at everyone who was there. "I'm so sorry, Andrew and Emma. I never meant to ruin your day like this. I just wanted to go for a walk. I don't know what I was thinking..." her words trailed off as she covered her face with her hands.

Her step-brother walked over, putting his hand on her shoulder as he crouched down to talk to her. "Beth, you didn't ruin anything. We won't let anything happen to you. Stewart Barlow can holler all he wants. I assure you there is no judge in the country who will take the side of a man who attacked a woman. All I know is that Hank Barlow is lucky I wasn't the one who came in and caught him. He would have suffered a lot more than he did."

Beth tried to offer him a smile, then looked up to Nate. "So, I guess you have to arrest me." She looked so small sitting on the cot, all Nate wanted to do was pick her up and run away some-where where she'd be safe. But he knew if he didn't handle things as he was supposed to, Stewart would get someone here who would arrest her, and then everything would be out of his control.

At least here, he could make sure she had a fair trial, and he could keep her safe.

"I'm afraid so, Beth. I don't want to, but if I don't, there's no telling what Barlow will do." He turned to explain to the others. "At least here, I can keep her out of his hands, or anyone else he could pay off. She'll be assured a fair trial with Judge Andrews when he comes back around in a few days' time."

In all his years of being a sheriff, he'd never hated his job more than he did at this moment.

"Nate, can you please just hurry and get me back to the hotel. I'm tired and need my rest." He'd forgotten all about Susan. He assumed she'd followed the crowd when they came over, but he hadn't even noticed her standing there.

Sensing his anger growing, Sarah walked over to her and told the woman she'd take her back to the hotel since she and Jake were heading there now. Before she left, she went over and hugged Beth. "Don't worry, little sister. I have no doubt in my mind that Nate will take good care of you." She stood up and met his eyes. He knew she was telling him he better take good care of her sister, or he would be answering to her.

The others all said their goodbyes, letting Beth know they were all behind her. No one was going to let her pay for something that Hank had caused himself.

When the last of the family left, Nate pulled his chair over to the cot. Sitting down to face her, he asked, "Are you all right, Beth? Did Hank hurt you?" He looked in her eyes to make sure she told him the truth. Finally noticing the blood that was drying around her mouth, he reached up to wipe it off with his finger. As soon as he touched her lip, he felt the familiar lump form in his stomach.

Not able to take his hand away, he gently wiped until the blood was gone. He couldn't take his eyes off her lips. Realizing she'd been through enough tonight he pulled his hand back like he'd been burned.

Finally, she answered. "I'm all right Nate. He didn't hurt me." She rubbed at her wrists where he could see bruises starting to show on her skin.

Standing up, he pushed the chair back and ran his hands through his thick hair. "I swear Beth, when I saw Hank on top of you, I thought I'd kill him myself." Turning toward her, he added, "I promise I won't let you pay for this. I saw what he was doing to you." He shook with anger as he replayed it over in his mind.

"I know you'll help me, Nate." She smiled at him. "So, I guess I'll be sleeping here now too? Guess I'm lucky I cleaned everything up so nicely since I'll be spending some time here." She tried to lighten the mood, knowing how hard it was for him to have to arrest her.

Standing up to walk into the tiny cell in the corner of the room that normally only housed the drunks as they fought on the streets after a night at the saloon, Beth held her head high, closing the barred door behind her with a loud clink. "Better make sure you get the key and keep it well hid so I don't escape." She was putting on a brave face, but he wasn't fooled.

He could see the pain in her eyes, and he desperately wanted to see the spark he was used to seeing. He needed to fix this.

He cursed again as he walked over to lock the door. Looking in her eyes, he said, "I give you my word, Beth, I will not let Stewart Barlow win. I will get you out of here. Do you trust me?"

He felt like his heart would stop beating as he looked in her eyes. Smiling at him, she quietly replied, "I would trust you with my life, Nate."

He reached his hand through the bars to touch her cheek, then turned to make his own bed up on the cot she'd been lying on.

"What are you doing?" she asked him.

"You don't think I'd leave you alone in here?" He sat down and took his shoes off, then lay down on the cot with his hands behind his head. "I'd be scared you'd break out somehow and head out to Stewart Barlow's to take things into your own hands." He smiled as he heard the familiar sound of her huffing at his assumption she'd try something like that.

"I think it's safer for everyone if I just stayed here and kept you company." He didn't want to admit that he would never leave her alone here with Stewart Barlow still around. He didn't trust that man, and there was no way he'd leave her to face another Barlow on her own like she did tonight.

He decided he'd waited too long to make Barlow pay.

CHAPTER 6

Beth lay on her small cot, listening to the even breathing of the man still asleep on the cot across the room. She didn't want to move, giving away the fact that she was awake.

Staring at the ceiling as the first rays of the morning sun started to break through the windowpanes, she tried to make sense of everything that'd happened. Unable to sleep last night, she'd tossed and turned, trying not to bother Nate who she'd hoped was sleeping better than she was.

She kept playing the scene over and over in her head, wondering if she could have done anything different. How had she let herself get cornered by that snake anyway? She'd been so lost in thought that she hadn't even heard him come into the stables, giving him the advantage.

She cringed as she remembered the feeling of his hands on her, and the smell of his breath as he tried to kiss her. Unable to hold it in, a small cry escaped her lips as she recalled the moment he'd pushed her to the ground.

Instantly, she heard Nate's cot squeak as he jumped up to come check on her. Closing her eyes tight, she pretended she was still sleeping, not ready to face the day ahead.

"I know you're awake, Beth." She had no idea how the man could go from sound asleep to up and alert so quickly.

She peeked one eye open to see him standing there, leaning against the wall. He was smiling, holding his arms across his chest.

"Don't you ever sleep?" She felt grumpy, not having had enough sleep. "And do you just sleep with all your clothes on, or did you manage to dress on your way from your cot?"

He laughed. "Yes, I slept quite well considering the amount of squeaking I heard from your cot as you flopped from side to side. And I normally sleep in the nude, if you really want to know, but I didn't think you'd want to have a naked man lying across the room from you." He wiggled his eyebrows up and down in her direction, while he pushed himself away from the wall.

"I assume you'd like some privacy so you can freshen up?" He walked over to the corner of the room where a stove sat. He dipped a large pot into a bucket of water beside it and set it on the stove to heat up.

"What I would like, is a change of clothes and something to eat." She wasn't sure why she was feeling angry, and she felt bad taking it out on Nate. He'd been so kind to her, and she knew she wasn't mad at him. She was mad at the circumstances she found herself in.

"I'm sorry Nate. I don't mean to be so foul." She sat up on the edge of her cot, trying to press at the wrinkles on her clothes while pulling the hair that was falling around her face back up into her bun. "I guess I didn't get much sleep last night."

He stood watching her. "No, I imagine you wouldn't have." Before he could say anything else, the door flew open and Sarah and Jake came in.

"Beth, how did you sleep? Are you all right?" Noticing Nate standing there, she raised an eyebrow. "You're here mighty early this morning."

"Did you think I'd just leave the office door wide open for anyone to race in here and help her escape? I know what you women are like in this family, and I wasn't taking any chances." Jake laughed at Nate's comment, getting an elbow in his ribs from his wife.

"I told you, I'll take care of this mess. But I need you all to promise to trust me and let me do things by the law. We can't let Stewart Barlow get anything else he can use against Beth." He was looking at Sarah, knowing that if anyone was going to do something to get Beth in deeper trouble, it'd be her.

Sarah lifted her chin, then turned to face Beth. "I brought you a change of clothes, and Momma is making you some breakfast. Everly is going to bring it over."

Beth noticed Nate looking toward Jake. "Well, now that Beth has someone here to sit with her, I'm going to take your husband, and we'll take care of everything over at the stables."

Her face drained of blood as she realized Hank's body was likely still lying in the stables. Nate's eyes met hers, and he gave her a smile. "We won't be long. You and Sarah can visit while you get cleaned up. I put a pot of water on to heat up,

Sarah, and there is a wash basin by the cupboard in the corner."

Beth watched them go out the door, while Sarah tried to keep her mind on other things. But all she could think of was the blood that'd been coming from Hank's head, and knowing that now, because of her, Nate was having to clean up her mess.

◎◈◎

SHE'D BEEN LOCKED in this cell for three days. Well, to be fair, she wasn't really locked in all the time. If Stewart ever found out, she knew Nate would pay, but during the day, he let her out of her cell to walk freely around the office.

She kept doing the work she'd been hired to do, hoping it would help her to pass the time. Nate had tried so hard to make things more comfortable for her, and she felt bad knowing how much he was doing for her. She knew he had even sent word to the judge asking him to come earlier than he was scheduled, but she still wasn't sure when that would be.

Both her sisters and their husbands had stayed in town. She had no shortage of visitors, and when they came around, Nate would go and tend to his other duties.

She knew he was also spending time with Susan, getting to know the woman he'd been writing to. She tried not to let herself think about him being with her, but she had little else to occupy her thoughts. So, she too often found herself wondering if they were starting to talk about their future, or if they were even falling in love.

Susan was a beautiful woman, and Beth had seen the way every man looked at her. She was petite and delicate, everything a man wanted in a woman. She'd likely never punch someone in the nose.

"Beth, are you even listening to me?" Her sister's voice intruded on her thoughts.

"Oh, I'm sorry Sarah! I guess I'm just so tired. It's hard to sleep on that cot." She flung her hand in the direction of her cell to point out the object she was speaking about.

"Seems more to me like you're thinking about something, or someone, else." Sarah had that look on her face like a cat that'd just swallowed a bird and hadn't got caught.

"I said, I've noticed Nate spending some time

with Susan over at the hotel. She seems to be settling in a bit better, although she still doesn't seem very happy about being here. I wonder why she'd even have bothered coming out here when she really doesn't seem to be the type to want to live in the Wild West, as she calls it."

Sarah and Everly were both visiting her today while Nate had to run to High Ridge. He'd given strict orders that if Stewart Barlow or anyone else unfamiliar came to the office, to get Beth locked back up in the cell so she wouldn't get caught.

He'd also mentioned again that they needed to abide by the law, and not to try taking matters into their own hands, giving the sisters a look that showed he meant it.

They were sitting around talking like they used to do in their apartment back east. The memories caused Beth to feel a bit melancholy as she thought about how much they'd all gone through over these past few months, and how much their lives had changed.

"Well, personally I think Susan is an awful woman. Who comes out west to meet a man, wearing silk? And a parasol? What's that supposed to even do?" Everly had brought Thomas, her young baby who was just starting to crawl. She bounced him on her knee as she let the others know her thoughts.

Sarah and Beth looked at each other, bursting into laughter. "What? What did I say that's so funny?" Everly looked at them both like they'd just gone mad.

"Oh, Everly, it's just you. Just saying it like it is." Beth took her nephew from Everly's arms, turning in circles causing the young boy to squeal with delight.

"If I didn't know better anyway, I'd say Nate is much more smitten with you than he is with that woman!" Ever the hopeless romantic, Sarah let Beth know what was on her mind too.

"Sarah. We all know that Nate is just a family friend. Besides, if he was interested in me, why did he place an ad for a bride? He could've just told me."

"And what would you have said, Beth? You aren't exactly the type of woman he likely felt he could profess his undying love to."

"What's that supposed to mean?" She stopped spinning, causing Thomas to shout, "Mo' mo'," wanting more.

"Beth, you are the most beautiful single woman in this whole area, and yet you don't even notice the way men are drooling all over you.

Instead, you act like you're one of the men, going about and doing things that make men more scared of you than in love with you." Sarah had heard about the incident at the hotel. "How many women would give a man a bloody nose?"

Beth scrunched her face up at her sister. "He had it coming, Sarah. You would've done the same thing."

She set Thomas down to crawl around on the ground while she sat down in her chair. "And anyway, it doesn't matter what Nate does or doesn't feel for me. The fact is, now he has a woman here who's come all this way to see if they'll be suited for one another. He can't just send her home without trying." She looked out the window to see Nate walking Susan to the door of the hotel.

He bent over to kiss the back of her hand. Beth noticed she wasn't wearing her gloves anymore, so maybe she was starting to adjust to life out here after all.

"And there's no denying how beautiful Susan is. Nate would be a fool to send her away." She watched him place his hand on the other woman's back as she started to go up the steps into the hotel.

She wondered what they were saying to one

another. Shaking her head, she turned back to see her sisters both watching her intently.

"Looks like Nate isn't the only one who is smitten." Beth scowled at Sarah who sat across from her, grinning from ear to ear.

CHAPTER 7

Beth stretched as she watched Nate get the key from the drawer. As had been the routine for the past five days of her being held, he'd get the key and let her out as soon as she woke up. She knew he'd get into a heap of trouble if anyone ever found out, but he didn't seem to worry.

"The judge should be here before noon, so you'll want to get yourself cleaned up well. I'll take you over to the hotel so you can have a proper wash and get some new clothes to wear." The familiar clink of the lock followed by the creak of the door opening always made her smile.

He joked that he only bothered to lock the door at night to keep her from running off and doing something stupid. He also wanted to make sure no one could ever call her reputation into question by staying here with him, so he always made sure it was locked in case anyone ever happened to come in.

"Thank you. I'll hurry so you can get me back here and locked up again before he gets here." She smiled at him to let him know she wasn't angry with him for having to do so. She knew it bothered him.

"You'll be glad when I'm out of here so you can sleep in your own bed, and finally get some sleep." She knew he hadn't been sleeping well. The sounds of his cot creaking while he tried to get comfortable filled the office all night.

"I do look forward to my own bed, but I admit I'll miss the company." He winked as she felt her cheeks start to burn.

He grabbed his hat from the hook by the door, leading the way out into the sunlight. This was the first time she'd been outside since she was arrested, and the bright sunlight blinded her for a few moments. Reaching her hand up to shield her eyes, she felt Nate's hand on her back as he walked behind her.

Knowing he could land himself in hot water for letting her out to run home and clean up, she hurried to step down and across the street.

"What is that murderer doing walking the streets before she's even met the judge?" She heard the words yelled loudly, in a voice she immediately recognized.

"Barlow. I'm escorting the lady to her room so she can clean up before the judge arrives. It's nothing that concerns you." Nate was tense, she could feel it in his body walking close to hers. Bending his head down and whispering so only she could hear, he said, "Just keep walking. Don't even look at him. I don't trust him, and I need you to stay right close to me."

She hurried her steps up, crossing the street and heading toward the door to the hotel. "Well, I'll be standing here watching and making sure that harlot is back out here to face the judge. So don't be getting any ideas!" Stewart was racing to keep up with them.

As they got to the door, Caroline met them there pulling it wide for them to come in. As Stewart tried to follow, she moved in his way. "Sorry, but you're not welcome inside these doors. So, either you wait outside, or I'll have you arrested for trespassing." She shut the door on his stunned face.

They could hear him hollering outside the door, but Nate just moved to stand directly in front of it, preventing him from entering. "Get upstairs and get yourself ready." He gave Beth a smile, not showing any of the tension she knew he was feeling.

Racing up the stairs, she hurried to her room to clean up. She needed to look presentable when the judge came. She'd met Judge Andrews and she knew he was a kind man, but she also knew he'd have to uphold the law. If Stewart Barlow had his way, she would be facing the gallows.

She tried not to let those thoughts creep into her head. Nate had spent the past few days assuring her he wouldn't let anything like that happen. For some reason, she completely trusted him.

She smiled as she thought back on the past few days. They'd spent so much time together, talking and getting to know each other. He was always the perfect gentleman, and he always seemed to enjoy riling her up and watching her lose her temper.

She had to admit that as much as she'd be glad to be free, she was going to miss being around him so much. If the judge let her go today, even though she'd still be working in Nate's office from time to time, she wouldn't be able to be there every day.

Fumbling to do up her dress as quickly as she could, her hands came to a stop as she looked in the mirror at herself. She realized she might have feelings for Nate she hadn't expected.

She sat down on the chair in the corner of her room, gathering her thoughts before heading down for the day ahead.

How had this happened? Had she fallen in love with him?

She knew every time he left to go spend time with Susan, she felt like her stomach had sunk right down to her toes. She knew she felt safe hearing his breathing at night, knowing he was there to make sure she was looked after. And she felt he was the one person she knew in her heart was going to do everything in his power to keep her safe today.

Standing to look in the mirror one more time, she tried to tame her hair the best she could. She realized as she did, she wasn't only trying to make herself presentable to the judge.

Her hands shook as she realized today was one of the scariest days she was going to have to face in her life. Not only was she going before a judge, who would decide her fate, she'd also realized something that almost tore her heart in pieces.

She'd finally fallen in love, but it was too late. He had a woman who he hoped to marry, and she had to honor that commitment he'd made. She owed him that after everything he'd done for her.

She realized that, after today, she'd have to somehow keep her distance from the man she desperately wanted to spend every minute with.

⚜

SHE SAT QUIETLY, hands crossed in front of her, as the judge got seated in the chair behind Nate's desk. She could feel herself trembling, until she felt Nate put his hand on her shoulder. He was standing just behind her. The only people Judge Andrews had allowed in the office were Nate and Stewart.

She knew her family were all waiting outside, but in here, if Nate hadn't been here, she'd have been terrified.

The judge hadn't been happy when he pulled into town, and had to face an angry Stewart yelling about his son being murdered, and how the sheriff wasn't doing his job, letting the accused walk freely around the town.

Nate had already sent word to the judge about the incident, which was why he'd come back earlier than he was scheduled. But, when Stewart started shouting as soon as he got close to the sheriff's office, causing Beth's family to start hollering back at Barlow, he hadn't been amused.

"Now, I want everyone to just sit down so we can sort this out." Judge Andrews was still angry. Nate pulled a chair up beside her, but Stewart obviously didn't feel his words applied to him, as he remained standing and glaring at Beth.

"There's nothing to sort out, Judge. This woman killed my son, and I expect her to pay for her actions. Just because the sheriff is getting in her skirts and doesn't want to follow the law, doesn't mean I'll stand for it!" His face was a mottled red color, and he looked like he hadn't washed in days.

She felt Nate tense beside her at the accusations Stewart was making. Wanting to stop him from saying anything that would get him in trouble, she spoke to the judge. "Judge Andrews. I'm sorry that you had to come out here to deal with this matter. I assure you, the sheriff has been following the law, arresting me as was needed after the incident." She looked towards Stewart, watching his lips curl up in a snarl as he looked at her.

Facing the judge again, she continued. "I did

kill Hank Barlow, but I was only defending myself from his attack."

The judge raised his eyebrows, looking towards Nate. "Can you tell me more of what happened?"

"He doesn't know anything! He wasn't there! I can tell you what happened. This whore lured my son to the stables, then killed him when he tried to show his affection!" Stewart was blinded by rage, not wanting anyone else to have a chance to speak. As she watched him, she realized he truly believed his own lies.

"Enough! I asked the sheriff for his side of the story, and I will get the chance to hear it." The judge slammed his hand on the desk as he made it clear to Stewart he was done being patient with him.

"Sheriff Dixon, what did you see?" He kept his eyes on Stewart, making it clear he was not to be interrupted.

"I walked into the stables, and I saw Hank on top of Beth. He had his hand on her mouth, but I could see her struggling." His fists were clenching, and she could see his jaw twitching as he started to get angry remembering what he'd seen. "Before I even had a chance to react, other than calling her name to let her know I was there,

Hank reached down to undo his belt buckle. She pushed her hips up causing him to lose his balance on top of her."

He looked toward Stewart to make sure he heard. "She pushed him so she could get up from under him, and that's when he fell and hit his head on a rock. It wasn't done on purpose; she was only trying to get away from him."

"Lies! They're all lying. He's only saying that because he's been following this woman around like a randy bull for weeks trying to get in her skirts." Nate was on his feet before Beth had a chance to stop him. He had Stewart pushed against the wall, holding him by his shoulders.

The judge jumped up, racing to pull Nate off Stewart. "Dixon! Don't do anything stupid. Let him go."

Beth stood, wringing her hands. What had happened here? She could see her chances of going free slipping away as everything seemed to be falling apart.

"Nate! Please stop!" she begged him to listen, knowing if he did anything to Stewart in front of the judge, he'd likely be in just as much trouble as she was.

Finally hearing her, Nate let Stewart go, but didn't back away. "You know as well as I do what happened that night. Your sorry excuse for a son tried to attack this woman, and he paid for it with his life. I assure you, if she hadn't have killed him, I would have." He was right in Stewart's face, growling the words between clenched teeth.

"That's enough. I've heard just about all I need to hear. The only one who's shown any amount of restraint or good manners is this young woman." The judge turned his kind eyes to hers. "Beth, I have no doubt in my mind what happened to you that night, and I'm sorry you had to endure it." He turned to face Stewart and Nate.

"I trust Sheriff Dixon with my life, and if that's how he says it happened, I have no cause to believe otherwise. Seeing your performance here today, if your son was anything like you, sir, then I'm sure I can imagine exactly what happened."

Beth could tell the man was angry. He turned back to her, offering her his hand. "And, young lady, I'm sorry you had to spend any time locked up for merely protecting yourself from harm."

With that, the judge sat down to sign the papers in front of him, giving her the freedom to go. He said he didn't find her responsible for the death of Hank Barlow, deeming it an accident.

She saw Stewart head for the judge, yelling

obscenities and vowing revenge. Nate stopped him, pushing him toward the door.

Hearing the commotion inside, by now Jake was at the door pulling it open for him. As Nate pushed him out the door, Stewart was yelling to anyone who would listen.

"This isn't over! My son was killed, and I'll make you all pay for this." His face was an ugly shade of purple now, and Beth was afraid he'd gone completely mad. The look in his eyes scared her as she walked over to the doorway, watching as the men hauled him to his horse.

"You won't get away with this you floozy! I know what you did!" He was screaming now as they pushed him toward his horse. Trembling, she watched Nate grab him by the arm and twist it up his back.

He whispered something into Stewart's ear, then shoved him. Stewart, finally realizing he was outnumbered, hopped on his horse and raced out of town.

She tried to put on a smile, happy that the judge had seen the truth of what happened, but she couldn't get the look in Stewart's eyes, or the words he spoke, out of her mind.

She somehow knew he wasn't just going to let this go.

CHAPTER 8

"I don't like these eggs at all! They're so runny, how can you expect me to eat these?" Susan's voice carried to the corner of the room where Beth was cleaning a table after guests who'd just finished their breakfast.

Hurrying over to see what the problem was, she couldn't help but notice the twitch in Nate's jaw. She knew him well enough to know he was annoyed. For some reason, that thought made her smile.

"Is there something wrong, Susan? Would you like me to get you some new eggs?" She tried to sound like she was truly concerned when in truth she wanted to throw the eggs in the woman's face.

Since she'd been released a few days ago, she'd been forced to spend a great deal more time with

73

the woman who was staying at the hotel. She tried to make her feel welcome and comfortable, but no matter what she did, Susan complained. Beth had no idea why she'd come out west when she was obviously never going to be happy here.

But she didn't want to ruin Nate's chances if Susan was who he wanted to be with, so she tried her best to make her see how wonderful it could be here if she gave it a chance. Even though she finally admitted it was breaking her heart to see Nate with another woman, she had to consider the fact that Susan had come all the way here to get to know him. Nate wasn't the type of man to throw away that kind of obligation lightly, so she knew he'd continue to try making things work with Susan.

"Beth, these eggs are awful. How could anyone eat them when they're so runny?" She almost looked like she was ready to cry, and when Beth looked at Nate, he was just sitting there with a look of shock as he watched Susan.

"I'll get you some new eggs, Susan. It isn't a problem." Turning to Nate, she gave him a smile of amusement, letting him know full well she was enjoying his discomfort. "Is there anything else I can get for you, Sheriff?" He scowled at her, having told her many times just to call him Nate.

He didn't look like he was enjoying his morning meal.

"Nothing, thank you, Beth. I have to get back to the office straight away, and if you aren't too busy today, there's a large pile of papers sitting for you to sort through. I think you've had enough time off to recover from your 'confinement'." He gave her an amused smile at her angry look. It was clear she didn't find it amusing to be accused of not handling her duties.

"I can't wait. I've certainly missed being around your warm personality all day." She shot him a radiant smile as she took Susan's plate to get her some fresh eggs.

Walking into the kitchen, she noticed her hands shook. She needed to get herself under control around him. She'd never been a simpering girl who blushed and fainted around men, so what was happening to her? It seemed now whenever she saw him smile at her, she felt her heart do a flutter down to her toes.

She looked out the opening into the dining room, and saw the couple sitting at the table. Watching them talking to each other, knowing they were getting to know each other better, made her stomach feel like there was a knife cutting into it. Why hadn't she realized how she felt about Nate before Susan ever got here?

Or was that what this was about? Was she only jealous because he was paying attention to another woman besides her? Realizing she'd perhaps just taken him for granted the past few weeks she'd been living here, without understanding how she really felt, made her feel like weeping. She couldn't help but think she'd missed her chance at finding someone who she could love, and who she had no doubt would care for her with his own life.

Deciding she needed to figure out how to move on, letting him be with Susan, she took a deep breath to steady her nerves. Turning around with the new plate of eggs, she pulled herself together. Noting the vinegar her mother had sitting out to do the pickles later, she fought the urge to douse the eggs in it.

Imagining what the reaction would've been helped her to put on the sweetest smile ever as she carried the plate back out to the dining room.

❧❧

NATE SAT at his desk rubbing his eyes. It'd been a few days now since Beth had been released, but he still wasn't sleeping. In fact, if truth be told, he'd slept better knowing she was in the cot on the other side of the room than he did back in his own room in the boarding house.

He'd just got back from his breakfast with Susan, and he felt a headache coming on. He felt obligated to give her a chance since she'd come here to meet him, but she wasn't making it easy for him to like her.

He was sure he'd never met a more spoiled woman in his life, and try as he could, he couldn't make out why she'd been in such a hurry to get here. If he'd been able to write to her a few more times, he was sure he'd have seen the kind of woman she was, saving her the trip out here.

Remembering the look on Beth's face as she pretended to sweetly take the plate from Susan to get the new eggs, he had to smile. She wasn't good at hiding her emotions. While she put a smile on her face, the look in her eyes gave her away. He could tell she was biting her tongue, and had laughed inside while he watched her hold it in.

He wondered why she did. It wasn't like Beth to keep her thoughts to herself. Hearing the door open, he lifted his head from his hands to see the woman he was thinking about walk in. He noticed her hair that always seemed to have a few pieces flying out with a mind of their own, and the color in her cheeks.

She was smiling, and he saw how her eyes lit up when they landed on him. Or maybe he imagined seeing something he wished to be true.

"Reporting for duty, sir!" She pretended to act serious as she walked over to the table he'd set up for her to sort through the papers. Looking around the room, she commented, "I see you've let the place go a bit in my absence. Looks like I'll be busy for a while."

He pretended to look shocked as he looked around. "I hadn't noticed!" The truth was, he hadn't felt like even being in his office much when Beth wasn't there, so he knew he'd let things go a bit. And, he'd had to hold a prisoner who had way too much to drink and was causing a disturbance, which had left a bit of a mess in the cell.

Watching her sit down, taking off her shawl and placing it over the back of the chair, he smiled. He couldn't understand it but having her here had helped his headache immensely.

They worked in silence for a while, and he caught himself looking over at her. He smiled as he saw her brows crease up in concentration as she read a paper and tried to decide where it needed to be put. If she was concentrating really hard, her teeth would pull her bottom lip in to bite it.

He felt his body react whenever he saw her biting her lip, and he had to keep looking away.

He had to remember he had another woman here he needed to give a chance. Pining over a woman he knew would never return the feelings wasn't going to help.

Once again, he heard the door open. Not expecting anyone else, he quickly lifted his head to see who it was. Ever since Stewart had made those threats after the hearing, he was on edge about him coming back for revenge against Beth.

The woman he saw standing there caused his jaw to hit the ground.

"Aunt Jenny? What are you doing here?" He jumped to his feet, closing the distance to the door before it even had time to shut behind her. "Why didn't you tell me you were coming? I would have met you."

His Aunt Jenny had taken him in and raised him after his mother sent him away the night Stewart had beat him so badly. His mother had taken him to see the doctor in town, getting his wounds tended to, then gone straight to the train station and bought a ticket to send him to Montana where her sister lived.

She'd sent a letter with him and arranged with another woman traveling that way to help get him where he needed to go. He would never forget that night, the fear in his mother's eyes, knowing she had to get him to safety.

And he'd never seen her again. After that, Jenny had raised him.

"Oh, Nate, for goodness sakes. I can get myself to where I need to go without your help." She slapped him gently on the shoulder, then grabbed his arms with both hands and pulled him in close for a hug. He picked her up and spun her around as though she weighed no more than a child.

Laughing, she hit him again on the back. "Nate! Put me down this minute! This is no way to treat a fragile, delicate woman!"

He laughed out loud as he set her down. "Fragile as a rattlesnake maybe!"

By now, Beth had walked over to where they were having their reunion. Noticing the young woman standing there, Jenny quickly looked her up and down, seeming to assess her worth within less than a minute. "And who is this lovely vision you have hidden away in here with you, Nate?" She put her hand out to Beth. "My name is Jenny. I'm this ruffian's aunt. And you are?"

Nate noticed how relaxed Jenny made people feel, and Beth was no exception. She put her hand out to take Jenny's. "My name is Beth Wilder. I help Nate out around the office a bit." She gave his aunt one of her dazzling smiles, and immediately Jenny was looking to him with a raised eyebrow.

"She's just a helper? Haven't you got eyes in your head?"

"Aunt Jenny." He gave her a warning look, not liking the way her thoughts were heading. "Beth is a friend who lives in the hotel across the street that her mother owns. She helps me here from time to time. That is all." He emphasized the last words, giving her the hint that he wasn't going to listen any more about it.

"Hmpph. Well, suit yourself. You never were the brightest of kids." She walked over and sat down in the chair that Beth had just vacated. She looked exhausted.

"Can I get you anything, Jenny? My Momma has the hotel, and I could run and get you something nice and refreshing to drink, maybe something to eat?" Beth asked.

"Oh dear, a cold drink would be lovely, thank you." As Beth raced out the door to get her something, she quickly raised her eyebrows in Nate's direction again.

"Don't say a word, Aunt Jenny. I don't want to hear it." He pulled his own chair closer to hers. "Besides, I have a woman who's come out from back east with the assumption we might get married. Her name is Susan, and she answered an ad I put for a woman to come west for marriage."

"What kind of fool thing have you done to end up with some strange woman coming here to marry you, when it's as obvious as the eyes in your head that you fancy that girl who just ran across the street? And, unless my eyes have finally caught up with my age, that girl only has eyes for you too." His aunt never beat around the bush when she had something to say.

"It isn't like that with me and Beth." He cut her off, not wanting to give her the chance to say anything else. He could see Beth coming back across the street with a pitcher of lemonade and some glasses. His aunt shrugged her shoulders, then took out one of the bags she'd dragged in the door with her.

"I had to come here as soon as I could, Nate. I found something I knew you had to see." She pulled out what looked to be a small notebook, with a woman's handwriting. She handed it to Nate, watching his eyes carefully.

Beth had come back in and was pouring them all a glass of lemonade. Nate couldn't even look at her as she set the glass in front of him. He recognized the writing in the notebook as his mother's. He'd seen a few cards and things around his aunt's house as he was growing up, and instantly knew it was in her hand.

"You can keep the notebook, Nate. There are an awful lot of pages she wrote about missing you and other things I know you'll appreciate reading." She leaned over in her chair and put her hand on top of his. "But, son, you need to read the part I've marked here." She opened the book in his hand to a section that had a paper stuck out marking the spot she wanted him to read.

He read the words on the page, feeling like his insides were being ripped apart. He could hear the blood rushing in his ears, as the world around him started to spin.

He couldn't hear anything else around him as he turned the marked pages, reading the words that left his world shattered. From somewhere far away he thought he could hear Beth's voice calling him, but he was too far gone.

He stood up so suddenly from his chair, it fell

over backwards. He was having trouble focusing as he looked at the concerned faces on the women in the room with him.

"Stewart Barlow is a dead man." That's all he could say as he flung the door open and raced outside.

CHAPTER 9

"Nate, stop! What are you doing?" Beth raced out the door behind him, begging him to stop. She didn't know what he'd read in that notebook, but she knew if he got away before she could stop him, he would do something he'd regret.

He wasn't listening, rage consuming him as he headed to the stables where he kept his horse.

Jenny was racing behind, her legs much shorter than theirs but still trying to keep up. "Nate listen! You can't go out there and confront him. You have what you need now to make him pay, let the law handle it."

He stopped, whirling around to face the women. "I am the law. And I *will* handle it."

Beth grabbed him by the arm while he was

stopped. The dust from the street blew between them, and people walking by were stopping to see what the commotion was about.

"Please, Nate." She was scared for him, never seeing him like this before. She desperately wanted to get through to him, to help him get through the pain and fury she could see in his eyes. "Please, just stop and listen. I don't know what you read in that notebook, but you can't do something you'll regret. Don't give that man something else to destroy!"

"Listen to Beth, Nate." Starting to cry, Jenny had caught up and was begging him to listen. "I knew I shouldn't have shown you. I should've gone straight to the law and let someone else handle it." The plump woman sniffed, trying to hold the tears back.

Nate pushed his hand through his hair, obviously torn between the anger consuming him and seeing the two women he cared about trying to stop him. Beth knew he didn't like seeing his aunt cry, and it was tearing at his heart.

"Aunt Jenny, you read what was in there. I can't let him get away with this. He destroyed my life. He needs to pay!" Nate's voice was strained, and he stood in the middle of the street, shoulders heaving as the breaths he was taking indicated how hard he was working to control his anger.

Without thinking, Beth reached her hands up to his face, holding it to look directly at her. His eyes showed so much pain, she ached for him. "Nate, whatever it is, we'll sort it out. We will make him pay. But you have to think it through. Don't let him win by confronting him and doing something you'll have to pay for. Please, just come back to the office and we can figure out a plan."

She never took her eyes from his, holding his face still so he had to look in her eyes. She spoke with her eyes, trying to get through to him. She didn't know how long they stood there, just looking at each other, but finally, he reached his own hand up and covered hers on his cheek.

He closed his eyes, and she could tell he was wrestling with demons in his own head, and she hoped she was getting through to him. Finally, he opened his eyes, and she saw him give a weak smile. "Beth, you do know how to make a man stop and take notice, don't you?" His voice sounded tired, but she knew by his weak attempt to tease her that at least he was prepared to sit down and listen before doing anything that would end up coming back to haunt him.

She smiled, still looking deep in his eyes as

they stood on the street. "It's about time you took notice." She pulled her hands down from his face and pulled his arm to turn him around. She noticed Aunt Jenny standing to the side, watching them intently with a kind smile on her face. She mouthed the words "Thank you" to Beth as she finally got Nate turned and walking back toward the office.

When they got inside, she looked at Nate. "Can I read what got you so upset? Or would you rather it stay private?" She didn't want to force him to let her in on something that was obviously so painful to him, but she didn't know how she could help if she didn't know what it was about.

He just shrugged his shoulders and sat down in his chair, leaning forward and putting his head in his hands. "May as well. Everyone will know soon enough once I figure out what I'm going to do to him."

Beth looked at Jenny, who handed her the notebook she'd brought. "This is Nate's Mom's journal she kept. I just found it when I finally decided to go through some of the things that were sent after Marian passed away." Beth noticed Jenny give a quick glance to Nate, who immediately tensed.

Looking back to Beth, she continued, "I

hadn't been able to do it for so long, the pain of losing my sister was too much for me. It was hidden, tucked away in a jewelry box, under the bottom shelf. Of course, there was no jewelry left that'd been sent. Stewart kept all that, but I guess he figured the old box wasn't worth anything, so sent it with a few other items after her death."

She motioned for Beth to read it. She looked toward Nate, making sure he was all right with her knowing what it said. He was looking at her now, and he just nodded his head.

She opened to the first page that had been marked.

I miss my son so much, sometimes it feels like my heart will never be whole again. But now I know I did the right thing by him. I hope he can forgive me someday for sending him away, but I needed him to be safe. I plan on leaving myself soon, once the time is right. I fear for my life, especially now that I found something so horrible, I can't even think of it without feeling the tears streaming down my face.

I've made such a mess by letting myself marry a man who was only taking advantage of the pain I was going through at losing my love, my dear David. Stewart had been a friend, or so I thought, and I believed I could trust him.

Now, I find out what a fool I was. Today, while Stewart was in town, I thought I would clean. When I don't keep things clean enough, he hits me and makes me pay for not doing my work.

I found an old box under some papers in a chest he has in our room. I opened it and found a letter. The letter was from his brother and was dated back just shortly after my David was killed in a hunting accident.

But now I discover it wasn't an accident, and my heart feels so broken I'm sure it will never heal.

I knew Stewart had been there when it happened, as they'd been friends and often went hunting together for meat to get us through the months. But he always said David had been killed by his own gun as he was cleaning it. I never suspected otherwise, but the letter from Stewart's brother showed me the truth.

He asked if Stewart had got rid of the rancher, and if he'd managed to convince the wife to marry him. He talked about the plan Stewart had to finally take over and have one of the biggest ranches in this territory.

My David worked so hard to build this ranch, hoping someday his own son would be able to take it over. Now, Stewart has it and I know he plans to pass it on to his own son Hank. Stewart's brother planned to join him, but he was himself killed on his way west so never made it here.

I've never been so scared in my life. I put the letter away as soon as I read it, but my stomach feels like there's a hole gnawing at me. I've missed so many months of my Nate's life, and he's all I have left of David. I need to get to him. The ranch isn't worth the fight anymore.

When Stewart got home, it's almost as though he sensed somehow that I knew the truth now. I don't know if he could tell I'd been in the box, but the look in his eyes has me fearing for my own life. I need to leave now and will leave as soon as I can sneak away without him knowing.

If he ever finds out I know the truth, or that I plan on leaving, I have no doubt now that he will kill me.

I just hope I can find the courage and the strength to get away before he does.

Beth sat staring at the paper before her, feeling tears welling up in her own eyes. She couldn't bring herself to look at Nate, now understanding the pain he was feeling at what he'd read. She brought her hand to her mouth as a silent gasp escaped.

Looking up, she saw Nate watching her. She

couldn't hold the tears back, feeling one slide down her cheek. The man she was looking at had just found out the man he hated all these years, and who he'd always suspected of killing his mother, had killed his father too.

He'd read about the pain his mother endured at the hands of Stewart Barlow, and the fear she'd felt in her final days. She was sure it was killing him to finally see it written in his mother's own words, seeing the pain she was living through.

"Nate, I'm so sorry." She didn't have any idea what else she could say. Standing to walk over to where he was still sitting in his chair, now with his head back down in his hands, she crouched down in front of him.

"We'll make Stewart Barlow pay for this. You helped me, and now it's my turn to help you. He won't get away with this, I promise." She waited for him to look up. Noticing the tear on her cheek, he reached his hand out to rub it away with his thumb.

He smiled at her, raising an eyebrow. "Do you honestly think I'll be letting you get anywhere near that man? He's already hurt one woman I care about. I assure you he won't ever be getting his hands on you."

With that, he stood up, taking the notebook

to his desk. "And now, since you two won't let me go and hang the man from the nearest tree like I was planning to do, I guess I'll need to figure out exactly what I'm going to do with the information I have here."

Beth smiled, letting the words he'd said about women he cared about sink in. She wasn't sure if he'd even noticed what he'd said, but when she looked over to where Aunt Jenny was sitting with a grin covering her face, she knew she'd heard.

"Well, you can say what you like, but I *am* helping. I'm a big girl and can look after myself. So, let's both sit down and figure out what we're going to do." Giving him the sweetest smile she could as she walked over toward him, he looked at her with his eyebrows furrowing together in the middle.

Ignoring his sigh as she pulled her chair up beside him, she heard him mutter, "Why was I afraid you were going to say something like that?"

CHAPTER 10

"Beth dear, come and sit down with an old lady and help keep her company!" Beth smiled at Jenny's description of herself as an 'old lady', walking over to the table to sit across from her. Jenny was having her lunch alone, while Nate had to run to High Ridge for the day.

The woman was hardly old, likely not much older than Beth's own mother. She had lines on her face that showed the laughter she'd enjoyed during her years. There was also a look of someone who'd endured a great deal, coming out stronger on the other side.

"Old?" She raised her eyebrows at the woman as she took her seat, smiling in her direction.

"Well, maybe not so old as much as wore out."

Jenny winked at her. "Besides, with Nate running off to who knows where for the day, I have plenty of time to spend getting to know the woman who's stolen my boy's heart." She gave Beth the most innocent smile she could manage, while Beth tried not to choke on the sip of tea she'd been taking.

"Jenny, Nate and I have both told you there's nothing more between us than friendship. He has a woman here he was writing to, a woman he is getting to know before marrying her, remember?" Beth was sure Jenny just didn't hear anything besides what she wanted to hear, and it seemed she had it stuck in her head that Beth and Nate were in love.

The woman set her fork down, leaning back in her chair to quietly sit and look at Beth. It made her feel uncomfortable, and she could immediately feel her cheeks getting warmer as she sat under the older woman's stare.

"Beth, do you truly not realize how Nate feels about you?" She said the words quietly, as though she was dumbfounded that she understood something that Beth didn't.

"Well, I know he cares about me a great deal. e's always been so good to me. He gave me a job in his office to help me out, and when I was arrested, he went above and beyond to make sure I was looked after..." Beth tried to explain to Jenny how Nate was just concerned about her as any man would care about a friend, especially a woman.

But as she started speaking the words, she remembered little things. Like the way Nate had called her name when Hank was attacking her, the way he'd carried her to the office after and defended her against anyone who was going to threaten her, including Stewart Barlow.

She remembered the look in his eyes when he was asking her if she was all right that night, and she remembered the words he'd spoken recently about not having another woman he cared about getting hurt.

She thought of the other small incidents; the way he'd made sure she was cleaned up for her hearing; and sat beside her during it when she was so afraid, never once letting her ever feel like she was on her own. She thought of the times she'd caught him looking at her, his eyes smiling as they looked into hers.

Jenny was smiling as Beth's voice trailed off, her thoughts causing her to sit staring into space with her hand coming up to her neck. "Oh my...you don't think...?" She looked at Jenny for an answer.

The other woman simply smiled, nodding her head. "I *do* think. And I think if you were honest with yourself, you'd realize that you feel exactly the same way." She then picked up her fork and went back to eating as though she hadn't just said the most shocking thing Beth had ever heard in her life.

Just then, Susan glided in the door, smiling and happy. Beth looked at her suspiciously, never having seen her like this in the entire time she'd known her. She held something in her hand that was obviously making the woman elated.

"Beth! Oh Beth! I have the most wonderful news." She rushed over to where she sat with Jenny, barely taking notice of the other woman. Nate had introduced them the first night she was in town, but Jenny hadn't thought much of her, and had let him know that quite bluntly.

"I know this will sound terrible, but I hope you can help me. I don't know how to tell Nate, and I mean, I see how much he seems to like you, so I'm sure coming from you it'll be so much easier." Susan was stammering, and Beth was having a hard time understanding what she was talking about.

"Susan, tell Nate what?" Beth tried to get her to just say what she as getting at.

"Oh Beth, I did something awful. I only came out here to make someone else jealous. I never meant to hurt Nate, but I had to make my beau back home see that I was serious and grown up, ready to be married. I knew he'd come for me, he just needed to realize I wasn't going to wait any more." She didn't look like she was overly upset about the horrible deceit she'd played against Nate, seeming more concerned about making Beth understand about her reasons.

Beth could only sit there in shock, unsure what to even say. Susan continued, "I would never have married Nate, I'd never have let it go that far." She seemed to think that made it all all right.

"Anyway, I couldn't have married him. I'm with child, and I had to let my beau see how much he missed me, and how badly he needed to marry me. The threat of another man raising his child was enough to finally get through to him." She spun around, holding a letter close to her chest.

"He just wrote me a letter, sending me enough money for a train ticket back home!" She was giddy with excitement, while Beth still sat there staring at the other woman like she'd gone completely crazy.

Surely she wasn't serious? How could anyone be so happy at a time like this, when they just revealed the enormous deceit they'd pulled on another person?

"You'd better be lying to me about this, Susan. How could you do this to Nate?" Beth was starting to shake with anger at the realization of what this woman had done. She stood up, calmly walking to stand directly in front of her. "You need to tell him this yourself. Don't expect me to clean up your mess." She was angry and she didn't care who was witnessing it.

"But Beth, he likes you. He will be all right if you tell him. Like I said, it wasn't like I hurt him. I would never have let it get that far." Susan was backing up as Beth kept walking toward her.

"You never hurt him? You wouldn't have let it get that far? Nate tried his hardest to make things work with you, feeling he owed you. He gave up so much to spend time with you, trying to get to know you, feeling obligated because you came rushing out here." She held her hands tightly at her sides as she continued, her voice getting louder as she kept talking.

"He deserves better than you anyway. You're

nothing but a spoiled, selfish brat who doesn't even think about the consequences of her actions. You were never good enough for him. The sooner you get your bags packed and get out of this town, the happier we'll all be."

Susan just stood staring at her as though she was worried Beth had completely lost her mind. Finally realizing she was done she flipped her hair over her shoulder and turned to leave the room. By now, Jenny was beside Beth, holding her arm, obviously worried the younger woman was going to do some kind of bodily harm to Susan.

She patted Beth's arm, while they both watched the beautiful blonde walk into the hall and up to her room. Jenny led Beth back to the table, helping her to sit down. Beth was shaking she was so angry at what she'd just heard.

She looked at Jenny. "What are we going to tell Nate?" She hated the thought of having to break this to him.

"Oh Beth, I'm sure when he hears it coming from you, he'll be more happy to be rid of her." She patted Beth's hand on the table. "Trust me, he's far better off without that woman around. I just wish he'd found the truth out sooner.

"Now, finish your tea and let's talk about how we're going to tell him." She picked up her fork

again and resumed eating the rest of her meal.
Beth could only sit staring at her in confusion,
wondering how she could witness something like
what they'd just seen, and go straight back to
eating like nothing had happened.

Jenny truly was a remarkable woman.

BETH WAS CLEANING up the dining room as she
heard the door in the hall open and close. Taking
a look out the front window, she saw Susan
carrying her bags up the street toward the train
station. She couldn't help but notice the woman
didn't seem to have any trouble carrying them all
herself when she was heading home, in compar-
ison to her production when she'd arrived in
town.

Deciding she was going to make good and
sure Susan got on a train out of town, Beth
grabbed her shawl from the hook on the wall.

As she stepped out onto the wooden sidewalk
running along the street, she noticed Susan stop
and turn her head as though she'd been called.
The woman set her bags down, turning to go
toward the side street that went behind the hotel.

Beth had an uneasy feeling, wondering why

she'd have stopped and gone in that direction, away from the train station. She hurried her steps, rushing to catch up.

As she came around the corner, she was knocked to the ground as a horse sped past her. On the horse was Stewart Barlow, and being held in front of him, with his hand over her mouth, was Susan. They raced out of town, behind the hotel and in the direction of his ranch. Beth shouted for them to stop, hoping the fear of someone seeing him would stop him and force him to let the woman go.

She pulled herself back up to her feet, racing back to the hotel through the cloud of dust settling around her. As much as she hated Susan, she wasn't going to let anyone suffer at the hands of that monster.

She was going to have to help her.

CHAPTER 11

Beth threw the door open, racing into the hotel. Jenny was standing talking to her mother, and they both turned when they heard her come in.

"Stewart has taken Susan! He grabbed her on the way to the train station. Tell Nate when he gets back to come out and help us!" She could barely talk, trying to catch her breath as she handed her shawl to her mother. She turned back around so she could run to the stables and get a horse to follow Stewart.

Caroline grasped her arm, "And where do you think you're going? You can't go following him out there! Wait until Nate or someone else gets here who can handle it." Beth noticed the fear in her mother's eyes as she spoke, knowing her daughter was going to be difficult to reason with.

"Absolutely not! You listen to your mother. You're not going out there on your own." Jenny was putting her hand on her other arm.

Beth wrenched both arms free, backing up toward the door. "I'll be careful. We can't leave her alone out there with him. I promise I'll be careful. Just make sure you tell Nate to hurry."

Beth knew the moment that her mother realized she wasn't changing her mind. Caroline sighed, pulling on her arm as she walked with her toward the door. "I know there's no reasoning with you when you get something in your head. So, while you follow them, I'll head in the direction of High Ridge and try to meet up with Nate so I can get him headed in your direction faster."

Beth stopped moving, smiling at her mother when she looked back at her to see why she'd stopped. Her Momma had always been so strong, and now, just because there weren't any men around to help them, she wasn't going to just sit back and wait for one of them to come and help.

"Thanks, Momma. I knew I could count on you."

"Well, don't think I'm missing the party!" Jenny was clamped on to her other arm, pulling them all out the door. "No more wasting time. I'm going with you, while your Ma gets to Nate." Beth couldn't help the stunned look on her face as she now turned to face Nate's Aunt Jenny.

Without missing a step, Jenny raised an eyebrow in her direction. "What? You don't think I'd be letting the woman who has my Nate's heart run into a dangerous situation where she could be hurt, without some kind of back up?" She looked genuinely shocked that Beth would even think such a thing.

Shaking her head, Beth led the other women toward the stables. Even though she was thankful for the strong ladies beside her, she felt better knowing her mother would get to Nate and have him coming not far behind. Somehow, she just knew as long as he got to them, everything would be all right.

But, until he did, it was up to her to make sure Stewart didn't hurt Susan.

She just hoped she wasn't too late.

As they neared Barlow's ranch, they slowed their horses down, not wanting to give themselves away. She knew Stewart was likely on his own now that Hank was gone. He had some men who worked on the ranch at one time, but none of them would stay for very long after having to work for a man like him. So, she didn't think there'd be any of them to help him.

She hoped that between the three women, they could handle Stewart if they got caught.

They dismounted, quietly tying their horses near a creek where they could have some water and rest while she and Jenny walked the rest of the way. She knew they'd need the element of surprise if they wanted to get Susan out without anyone getting hurt.

"Beth, do you have a plan or are we just rushing in on a hope and a prayer?" Jenny's cheeks were red after the wild ride out here, and Beth had to smile at her offhanded remark. The woman was tying her horse, not even looking in her direction, her shoulders heaving as she tried to catch her breath.

"I don't know. I hope we can just sneak in, grab Susan and get back out without getting caught. Then, when Nate gets here, he can handle Stewart." Beth looked at Jenny. "Thanks for coming with me. But I know Nate would never forgive me if anything happened to you. So please, be careful!" She'd grown quite fond of

Nate's aunt, and she knew she would never forgive herself either if the woman got hurt because of her foolishness in following Stewart out here.

Jenny grinned, reaching her hand out to pat Beth's arm. "Oh dear, I'll be careful. But I must confess I wouldn't have missed the chance to catch the man who hurt my sister, and watch him finally pay."

Beth could understand how Jenny must be feeling. If anything ever happened to one of her sisters, she knew there'd be nothing on earth that would stop her from making anyone pay who hurt them.

Nodding at the other woman, she said, "All right then, Aunt Jenny. It's just me and you. Let's get Susan out of harm's way so that when Nate gets here, Stewart will finally pay for everything he's done to cause so many people pain."

"But you have to promise me that if anything happens and Stewart catches us, you will get Susan out of the way and get out of here. Nate can't be worrying about all of us when he gets here." Beth knew that if Stewart caught them, he'd likely make a grab for one of them since he'd know Nate would be more upset with him having one of them than he would be with Susan.

When he did get here, he wouldn't need the extra pressure of Stewart having them all in harm's way.

And, she had no doubt in her mind that when he did get here, he'd be rushing in like a madman, fueled by anger, so she needed to try and make things as easy for him to get to Stewart as she could.

By now, they'd snuck up to the edge of the property by the barn. Beth could hear a woman sobbing, hollering for Stewart to let her go. Susan wasn't making it easy on the man who'd grabbed her, if the sounds coming from the barn were any indication. Beth almost had to laugh knowing Stewart had likely had to endure listening to her squeal all the way from town.

And now he obviously had enough of listening to her. They watched him slam the barn door, while the woman inside was still screaming in a high-pitched voice to let her go, demanding he get her out of that filthy barn. Stewart stomped toward the house, obviously believing he had the advantage now, but not wanting to sit listening to the woman until Nate got there.

Beth knew he must have watched Nate leave town this morning, then waited for one of them to be alone so he could get to them.

She just wasn't sure what he was hoping to accomplish.

"I'm going to sneak in and get Susan out. You stay out here and watch for Stewart. If you see him coming back, you'll need to whistle and let me know." Beth was already moving toward the barn door, not even giving Jenny time to argue.

"You be careful, girl!" Jenny's voice hissed as she tried to be quiet.

Sliding through a small opening in the doorway, Beth got inside and waited for her eyes to adjust to the darkness of the barn. She could still hear Susan, so she knew exactly which direction to head.

"Let me out of here this instant, you monster! You'll pay for this! My dear Harland will have your head if you hurt one precious hair on my body!" Beth cringed, listening to the spoiled woman screeching at the top of her lungs. She reminded herself that even though she couldn't stand the woman she was here to help, no one deserved to be hurt at the hands of Stewart.

As much as she would've loved to walk away and let the woman pay for everything she'd done, she knew that wasn't the kind of person she was. She wouldn't let someone suffer if she could help it.

So, she headed in the direction of the noise, trying not to let Susan see her too soon, knowing she'd be apt to give her presence away.

When she got close enough for Susan to hear her, she whispered as loud as she could. "Susan. Don't stop yelling. I'm going to untie you and get you out of here." She moved behind the woman to start undoing the ropes Stewart had used to tie her hands behind the rough looking chair she was sitting on.

"Oh Beth! Thank goodness you're here!" Not even lowering her voice from the one she had been screaming with, Beth cringed again, hoping Stewart hadn't heard her. "Where's Nate?" She was looking around to see who else was there to rescue her.

"Susan! Will you keep your voice down? We don't need Stewart hearing you." Just then, Beth could hear the sound of a loud whistle breaking through the walls. Hurrying to undo the ropes, she started giving Susan instructions, knowing they were out of time.

"Run outside behind the barn. Jenny is there waiting. You guys need to get back to safety and wait until Nate gets here!" As the last knot was untied, Susan was already on her feet. Beth stood to turn and run behind her, but Stewart was already inside the door.

"Well, isn't this nice. I got myself two women." He was leering at them both as he crept his way closer to them. Beth noticed his eyes were completely mad, as though he'd lost touch with reality, with no emotion other than blind fury showing from their depths.

Susan started screaming loudly, causing him to falter. Beth took advantage of his pause, pushing Susan past him toward the door. She was right behind her, but she felt Stewart's grip on her arm before she could get by.

"Oh no you don't! You're the one person I know will cause Nate the most pain to see me hurting, so you'll be staying here with me. And, I have a score to settle with you." He was holding her arm so tightly she could feel sharp pain starting to radiate up to her shoulder.

He put his face right up to her ear. "He'll feel the pain I felt at losing my son as he watches me make you pay for what you did." His breath was hot, and as she fought the nausea at him being so close, he pulled her by the back of the hair and forced her head back.

"I'm going to finish what my son started, but

I'm going to make sure Nate is here just in time to witness it." With those words, he threw her to the ground. She quickly rolled to the corner farthest away from him. Her whole body shook, as fear from the night Hank attacked her rushed back.

He grabbed the rope he'd used on Susan and moved toward her. "You won't get away with this, Stewart. Nate is already on his way, and you will pay for everything you've done." She was not going to just lie down and let him win without a fight.

"We know what you did. We know you killed Nate's father, and we know you killed his mother. You're going to pay for all of it." She wanted him to know his past was catching up to him, hoping it would throw him off enough that she could escape.

He yanked her by the hair, pulling her to her feet. "You don't know nothing, you little hussy!" She noticed his eyes flicker with doubt as he turned her around, pushing her hard against the wall as he tied her arms together. When he was finished, he pushed her toward the chair she'd just freed Susan from.

She noticed he was starting to seem more agitated. She prayed her mother had got to Nate and he was on his way.

But the look on Stewart's face as he stood there panting, staring at her with lifeless eyes, made her hope he wasn't coming alone. She had no doubt that the man in front of her had every intention of hurting Nate.

At that thought, she felt a sob catch in her throat. Hearing it, Stewart grinned, knowing he had the advantage. The laugh he let out from his throat caused the hair on her neck to stand up.

She realized the man they were fighting now was completely out of his mind with madness. She'd never felt fear like she did now, knowing Nate was walking into a fight he might not be able to win.

CHAPTER 12

Nate raced towards Barlow's, fury burning in his veins. He didn't know if he was angrier about Stewart grabbing Susan, or if fear was causing him to feel an anger he'd never known before when Caroline told him Beth and his aunt had gone off after them.

Beth was the most stubborn, foolish woman he knew, and putting her together with his Aunt Jenny was a deadly combination.

He could hear the hooves behind him as Jake and Caroline raced to keep up. Jake had been riding back into town with him when Caroline had come racing up to them on the road.

When she told them what'd happened, he hadn't even stopped to think before kicking his horse into motion, not caring who followed or not.

He was going to strangle Beth when he got his hands on her, after he made sure she was all right.

Caroline was trying to tell him the rest of the story about Susan and explaining why she'd been on her way to the train station. Nate was hearing some of it as they flew down the road toward the ranch, but he didn't care. All he cared about at the moment was seeing if Beth was all right.

Now and then, he could hear Jake curse, as he heard the story. He was glad to have Jake with him, knowing he might have more of a situation with all the women in Barlow's hands than he would've if it'd just been Susan on her own.

But now, thanks to Beth, Barlow had an advantage.

As they got closer to the ranch, he saw two horses tied to a tree near the creek. His stomach knotted as he realized he was too late, and the fool woman had gone ahead to try and save Susan on her own. Clenching his jaw, he kicked his horse to go faster.

Coming around a bend, he almost ran over his aunt and Susan racing toward him. Startled, his horse reared up, almost knocking him to the ground.

"Oh Nate! Thank goodness you're finally here." His aunt was struggling to catch her breath, obviously upset. "Stewart has Beth."

"Dammit, Jenny! What were you two fool-headed women thinking coming out here on your own?" He was desperately trying to calm his spooked horse down so he could get to Beth.

Susan was shrieking, crying and carrying on so loud, it was all he could do not to slap her. "Susan! Stop it, you're scaring the horse." Jenny pulled hard on her arm, trying to get the woman to listen.

"What are we going to do Nate? How are we going to get her out of there?" Caroline had ridden up, hearing everything.

He looked in her eyes and could see fear, but he also sensed that she was angry and ready to get her daughter away from danger. Jake was dismounting, walking toward him.

"Just tell me what you want to do, and I'll be right behind you." Jake hated Stewart Barlow just as much as Nate, so he had no doubt he'd have his back.

Nate thrust his hands through his hair, having lost his hat miles back. "I honestly don't know." He was struggling to gather his thoughts, and the sound of Susan crying loudly wasn't helping his nerves. He finally had his horse calmed down, so he hopped back up in the saddle.

"All I know is, I'm going to make him pay. He's hurt too many people, and I'll be damned if I'll let him hurt Beth too." With that, he kicked his horse into motion, leaving Jake and Caroline racing to catch up.

❧❧❧

BETH SAT GLARING at the man who was pacing back and forth. The dust in the barn was heavy, causing reflections in the sunbeams that shone through the broken windows of the barn.

He was rubbing his hands together, every now and then looking over at her with a crazed look. "Don't you worry, son, I'll make this whore pay." Beth couldn't tell if he was talking to himself, or if he genuinely believed Hank was there with him.

He kept babbling as he walked over by the door, looking out, then heading back. "I don't know what Marian's crazy sister Jenny is doing here, but I won't be letting her spread any lies about me. I won't give up what I've fought so hard to get all these years." His voice was reaching a fever pitch, and Beth seriously worried he was going to lose his grip on reality at any moment.

Just then, the barn door flew open, and Beth could see the outline of Nate standing in the doorway. Her heart thumped in her chest as she worried about the confrontation she was about to witness.

Stewart instantly grabbed her, pulling her to her feet. He dragged her backwards, keeping his arm tight around her throat. She'd seen a knife back where the leather saddles were sitting, and she worried he was going to try and reach it.

Nate walked into the barn, still not having said a word. She could see his face now as he stood in the light from one of the windows. She could see how angry he was, but when his eyes lit on hers, for a moment, they softened.

"Are you all right, Beth? If Barlow has so much as laid a finger on you, he's a dead man." The calmness in his voice didn't fool her. He was barely holding his anger in check, and she knew he was fighting to keep it under control until he got her away from Stewart.

Without taking her eyes from his, she answered. "I'm okay, Nate. He hasn't done anything." She tried to send him a message with her eyes to be careful, desperately wanting to let him know how much she loved him. She was so afraid she wouldn't have the chance to ever tell him.

He kept his gaze locked on hers, until Stewart broke the silence with a crazed laugh. "I knew you'd come for her. I knew I could get you here." He pulled his arm tighter around Beth's neck. "Now, you'll see how it feels to have someone you love get hurt right in front of your own eyes!"

He kept backing away. Nate kept walking toward them. Beth recognized the book he pulled from the inside pocket of his jacket. "You mean like you did to my father? And my mother?" His voice was so low, Beth almost couldn't hear him. He waved his mother's notebook in front of Stewart's face.

"Don't you think you've hurt me enough? You had the ranch, you got everything. But you just couldn't let it be enough." Beth could see the fury building in Nate's eyes.

"What...what's that? How do you know?" Stewart's voice wavered. "You don't know nothin'!" he spat the words from his mouth.

"Oh, I know plenty. And, I have a book written in my own mother's handwriting to prove it. You're done, Barlow, and now it's time for you to pay." Nate wasn't backing down, causing

Stewart to pull Beth in front of him, almost cutting her breath off as he tightened his grip around her throat.

Beth could see Jake standing in the doorway now, and her mother behind him. Stewart must've seen them at the same time, growling low in his throat, "Stay back!" He frantically looked back toward Nate, eyeing up the book he was holding.

"I don't believe you. There's nothing in that book. Let me see it."

"I'm not giving it to you, unless you let Beth go. Let her go, and you and I can settle this away from the law."

Realizing he was going to give up the proof he needed to put Barlow away, Beth cried out to him, "Nate, no! Don't let him have it!"

He didn't even glance in her direction, pretending he didn't hear her. He was holding his gaze on Stewart, waiting to see his decision. He threw the book on the ground at Stewart's feet.

The moment she felt his grip loosen, she elbowed him as hard as she could in the ribs, giving Nate the advantage he needed. She moved out of the way, feeling Jake grab her arm to pull her to safety as Nate went for Stewart.

While Jake untied her arms, they could hear the sound of the other two struggling against one another, Stewart shouting crazily, confessing to everything. It was almost as though he was enjoying the fact that Nate was hearing everything that'd happened.

Nate had him on the ground, pulling his gun from his holster. "Time for you to pay, Barlow, I've been waiting for this for a long time."

Realizing what he was about to do, Beth ran over, clutching at his arm. "Nate, don't do it. Make him face the law with the proof you have now to make him pay." She was begging for him to listen, knowing he wouldn't be able to live with himself for killing a man in cold blood.

"Please, Nate. Don't throw your life away because of someone like him."

"Listen to your whore, Dixon. She's obviously got more sense than you." As he spoke the words, Beth caught a glimpse of his arm coming forward. Before she could warn him, she saw the glint of a blade as Stewart brought it up, slicing through Nate's jacket and drawing blood from his side.

"Let me give you another scar to remember me by." The words were shouted from Stewart's mouth, as Nate fell off to the side, clutching at his ribs. Jake had Barlow on his feet and face pressed into the wall before anyone else had a chance to react.

Beth rushed to Nate's side, grasping at his jacket to pull it apart to see his wound.

She could feel tears flowing down her cheeks, putting her hands all over his side trying to see where the blood was coming from. "Nate, are you all right? Oh, Nate, I'm so sorry! I shouldn't have distracted you. What have I done?" She was sobbing now, unbuttoning his shirt underneath, trying to stop the bleeding.

She felt Nate's hand come up, stopping hers. She lifted her eyes to his, noting the look of pain on his face. "Beth."

All he said was her name, but he said it with so much love, she was sure she'd burst. "Nate, you'll be all right. Just let me find where he cut you." She knew her voice was shaking with fear, and she couldn't stop the tears that were now falling onto his chest.

"It's just a nick...I've had worse." He tried to make a joke, but she was too upset to find it amusing.

She felt his hand come up to her cheek, rubbing away the tears that were leaving a trail through the dirt she knew was covering her face. She pressed her face into his hand, closing her eyes to enjoy the emotion that she was feeling in the warmth of the hand holding her.

"I love you, Beth." Her eyes flew open as she heard the words. More tears started flowing, as she sobbed, hoping he wasn't saying the words knowing he was going to die.

"Nate, stop! You're going to be fine. Please, just don't die on me!" She was again frantically trying to find the wound, finally pulling his shirt back enough to see that it was, in fact, just a small cut that would heal. She realized there wasn't really as much blood as she'd thought in her fear.

Crying with happiness, she flung herself onto his chest, throwing her arms around him. She noticed the smile on his face as she finally realized he wasn't hurt as badly as she'd thought. "Nate, if I wasn't so worried about you right now, I'd seriously hurt you for scaring me like that!" As she landed on his wound, she felt him flinch.

"Ouch! Woman, you're going to be the death of me." She felt his arms come up around her waist.

Pulling herself back, not wanting to hurt him anymore, she reached her hands up to hold each side of his face. She looked in his eyes as she finally told him the words she'd been longing to say for so long. "Nate Dixon, you're the most infuriating, stubborn and hot-headed man I know. But I love you."

She lowered her head to his, placing her lips on his. She felt his arms tighten around her waist, hearing a low moan in his throat as his mouth took over hers. As he kissed her, she felt like the world around her was spinning. The longing in his kiss told her everything she needed.

Lifting her head, she felt the heat as his eyes bored into hers. "Don't ever scare me like that again. I could've lived with everything else, but the thought of losing you was more than I could stand. You have my heart, Beth Wilder, as you have since the first day I saw you running across the street when you arrived in town." His hand reached up to brush her hair away from her face, then letting his fingers slide down to her mouth.

He smiled. "I just wish I hadn't had to lock you up to make you see that you loved me too."

Hearing a throat being cleared, they realized everyone was still standing there. Jake was hauling Stewart toward the door, as Caroline stood waiting for the couple on the ground to get back up. Stewart was still yelling nonsense, trying to fight against Jake.

As they went past where Caroline stood, Stewart was able to wrestle himself free. Seeing her standing there, the man lunged at her, making one more last-ditch effort to make someone pay.

"If I can't hurt the whore who killed my son, I can hurt her mother!" He screamed the words as he reached her.

Beth watched in horror, as he came at her mother. Caroline turned, pulled her arm back and connected squarely on Stewart's nose.

Blood started to gush from his face, as he reached up to tend to his now twice-broken nose.

"Nobody calls my daughter a whore." With those words, she brushed her skirt off, then turned to walk toward Beth and Nate. Jake held Stewart on the ground, tying his arms up with the rope.

"Momma!" Beth ran to her mother, who took her in her arms. She pulled back, looking in her mother's eyes. "You know, that wasn't very lady-like." Caroline just smiled and shrugged, while Beth laughed.

Bending down to help Nate to his feet, he pulled her down onto his lap. He pulled her in for another kiss, bringing his arms tight around her waist. "I've never been so scared in my life as I was when I knew you were in danger. Promise me you won't do anything this stupid again. You could've been killed."

His eyes searched hers, desperate for her to promise she'd be careful so he wouldn't have to face losing her. As she looked in his eyes, the immense love she felt for this man overwhelmed her. She realized how long she'd been holding her feelings inside, and as she felt the heat from his gaze holding hers, she knew she'd finally found that love she never thought would be hers.

It had been right in front of her eyes all along.

Gently kissing Nate, she pulled back, holding her hand on his chest. "I can't promise I won't ever do anything stupid like this again, because we both know that would be a lie." She noticed the smile that reached up to his eyes.

"But I will promise you my heart, for now and forever."

Nate pulled her to him. "That's all I've ever wanted."

EPILOGUE

"Well, Mrs. Dixon, can I have this dance?" Nate bowed low before her, offering her his arm.

Smiling, she took his hand, letting him pull her up into his arms. The guests around them smiled as they watched the newly married couple dancing, holding each other so close it was like no one else was there.

Everything had returned to normal, or as least as normal as it could get, in Mulder Creek. Stewart Barlow had been sent back east to face trial for his crimes, and Nate had got the ranch back. As Beth looked around the yard, now filled with friends and family sharing in their special day, she couldn't help but feel the presence of Nate's parents.

Smiling up at her husband, she said, "You've made me the happiest women in Wyoming."

He smiled down at her, putting his lips down to hers in a gentle kiss. She reached her hand up to trace the line of the scar on his face. "And from here forward, no more living with the horrors of our pasts affecting our future." She loved this man, scars and all.

He cupped her hand in his, then pulled it to his mouth to place a kiss on. "Have I told you today how much I love you?"

She smiled. "Only a handful of times, but you know I never grow tired of hearing it."

As soon as Nate had got his father's ranch back, he'd spoken to Beth's brothers-in-law about joining the ranches to work together. With the stock of both, they now covered the majority of the Wyoming territory.

Caroline was now happily married to Alistair McConnell and was running a successful hotel and restaurant in Mulder Creek, while Beth's sisters were happily married and living in High Ridge.

Andrew and Emma had built a place not far from Nate's, and now Andrew was helping him to get into the swing of being a rancher, while he continued to act as sheriff in the territory between Mulder Creek and High Ridge.

Beth sat on a bench on the side of the house, watching everyone around her. She couldn't believe how far they'd all come. Seeing her sitting alone, her sisters, Sarah and Everly, walked over to sit beside her. The girls sat quietly together, each enjoying the moment. Caroline walked over to join them.

"Who would've ever thought we would be this happy?" Caroline was the first to speak, looking out at the crowd who were sharing in the festivities with them. "We've come to a new town, and we've all got our new beginnings." She looked over at her daughters.

"I'm the happiest Momma in the world, seeing how wonderful you've each turned out to be."

Beth smiled at her mother, reaching her hand out to hold hers. "Well, we learned to be just like our Momma." She laid her head on her mother's shoulder.

The men, sensing the women needed this time together, stood talking at the corner of the dance floor.

"We may not have been an ordinary family,

but we've always had more love shown to us than most people could ever wish for." Everly held her hand on her now expanding stomach, as she looked over to her husband Ben, who was trying to get their son to stop stealing food from the table.

"And now we all have our happy ever afters." Sarah smiled, looking towards Jake who, sensing they were talking about him, looked over and gave them a raised eyebrow.

Finally deciding they'd taken his wife from him long enough Nate walked over and took Beth's hand. "Sorry ladies, but you've had her long enough. Now it's my turn." Beth smiled back at her sisters and mother over her shoulder as he dragged her toward the house.

"Nate! We can't just leave our guests!" Beth was mortified that he was making her leave her own wedding.

Nate stopped, drawing her into his arms. "Beth, I think they'll all understand." With that, he lowered his head, kissing her now with a passion she instantly felt fire up in herself. His lips pushed hers apart, and he held her so close she felt his body crushing hers. She heard herself moan, as she lifted her arms up around his neck.

Unable to stand it anymore, Nate lifted her

into his arms and started carrying her toward the house. This time, Beth didn't care who noticed. She loved this man more than anything in the world.

It was time for them to have their future together, leaving the past behind. She wrapped her arms around his neck while he carried her. Leaning in closer, she whispered, "Thank you, Nate, for loving me." She smiled up at him.

His steps faltered as he looked down at her. He stopped, letting her slide down until her feet were on the ground. Looking in her eyes, he brushed her errant hairs away from her face. "Beth, you've brought so much happiness back into my life. You have my heart from today and forever." Putting his forehead to hers, he whispered, "Thank *you* for loving *me*."

He picked her up again, racing toward the house.

Smiling, Caroline watched from the bench. Looking upwards, she closed her eyes as she spoke to herself. "Thank you, dear Thomas, for loving me enough to save me all those years ago. I'll forever love you for the daughters you gave me. I hope I've done you proud." Feeling a hand take hers, she opened her eyes to see her husband standing in front of her, smiling down at her.

She stood, letting Alistair take her into his arms. As she looked around, she realized the Wilder women had all found home.

She now believed happily ever after could happen to anyone, even a woman like her.

SPECIAL SNEAK PEEK AT: A GAMBLER'S HEART

AVAILABLE NOW!

CHAPTER 1

"Stop fussing with your dress and lift your eyes up. It's no wonder you've never been able to attract anyone. You're slouched over in the corner where no one can even see you."

Fiona sat perfectly still, reaching her hands out to press against her gown. She knew there weren't actually any wrinkles but it kept her from having to look out at the ballroom.

At her stepmother's words, she lifted her eyes and swallowed the lump in her throat as she took in the sight of the beautiful gowns all around her. They danced in and out of her vision as the men swept the lucky women around in their arms, twirling them around on the dance floor.

This was the third ball she'd been to in the

past few days and she'd only had a handful of dances. Even those had only been with some of her father's friends who surely felt sorry for her or men she'd rather not have been dancing with anyway.

She'd had her coming out ball over two years ago, so the only men she was attracting now were the less desirable catches who knew their choices were limited.

Her stepmother had married her father after her mother died five years ago. He was an Irishman living in London and marrying a woman of Viola Dunning's status in society was considered quite an accomplishment.

That is, unless you were unlucky enough to be Fiona or one of her two sisters, Cora and Aileen.

Viola had two of her own daughters who were in the middle of their seasons and both were attracting all the right suitors. The possibilities were endless for the girls as they were courted vigorously by a selection of eligible men.

Cora and Aileen would have their seasons soon and Fiona had no doubt they'd have no trouble attracting matches for themselves. Both of them were beautiful, having inherited their mother's blonde hair that seemed to sparkle and change colors depending on the light.

Fiona was graced with her father's red hair and while it drew attention, it wasn't the kind a woman hoped to attract.

However, it wasn't only her hair that drew people's eyes to Fiona.

She'd been stained or blessed, depending on your point of view, with a red birthmark that stretched from the bottom of her jaw and down her neck. Her mother used to remark that it was in the shape of a heart and was a kiss from heaven.

But Fiona didn't feel that way about it. And it was apparent most other people didn't either.

The birthmark seemed to get redder when she was worried or under stress and the past two years had been full of both. She hadn't ever been prepared for a season in London, until her father had married Viola.

Now Fiona had spent her seasons watching others find suitors and become married while she still sat on the sides watching. She tried not to let it get to her but, the truth was, she was tired of feeling like she wasn't as beautiful as the other girls. She wanted to get as far away from all of this as she could but she didn't know how.

Standing, she held her hands clutched in front of her as she turned to Viola. "I think I will turn in for the night. I'm feeling so tired from the endless balls this week. I will send Miles back after he has dropped me at home." Miles was the family coachman who she knew would be waiting outside.

He would be a welcome face to see.

Her exit from the ballroom went unnoticed, she was sure.

"Good evening, Miss Fiona. Did you have a good night?" The servants all knew they could be friendly with her as she'd never gotten used to having others wait on her. She treated them all with kindness and they returned it to her.

His warm smile choked her up with emotion. He never looked at her like she was different and Fiona desperately needed to see a friendly smile after the night she'd spent watching everyone else have so much fun.

She smiled warmly at the older man as he held out his hand and took hers to help her into the carriage. "It was fine, Miles." She didn't trust her voice to say anything more.

He simply nodded at her, seeming to understand her need to avoid conversation about the evening. She looked out at the streets of London as they made their way back to the townhouse, watching other carriages go by, the sound of the horse's hooves clip-clopping on the cobblestones.

She missed the country. She wasn't a city girl. When her father had married Viola, they had moved to London, leaving her beloved country home behind.

She much preferred the solitude and the openness of the land. In the countryside, she could go outside and walk around in peace. She didn't have to deal with people who were initially drawn to the beauty of a young woman, quickly averting their eyes when they got close enough to notice the mark on her face. No matter how many times it had happened in her life, it still hurt.

The carriage pulled up to the front and Miles helped her down. She felt him give her gloved hand a gentle squeeze and she lifted her eyes to his.

"You were absolutely stunning tonight, Miss," he whispered the words to her so no one else would be able to overhear. She knew he was taking a risk speaking to her and it lifted her spirits to know he cared enough to take that chance.

She lifted her skirts and moved up the stairs to the house as fast as she could go, ignoring the servants who all bustled to help her as she came through the door. She just needed to get to her room where she could be alone.

Closing the door behind her, she knew it was only a matter of time until she had the maids coming to help her get changed and ready for the night. Something she'd always managed to do on her own up until she'd been forced to move to London.

She sat down at her dressing table, looking in the mirror at the girl staring back at her. Her skin was pale except for cheeks that were slightly flushed from the run up the stairs.

But when she turned her head to the side, she could see the birthmark standing out in bright red contrast to the white of her skin, despite the best efforts of the powder Minnie had applied.

Tears slowly made their way down her cheeks as she looked into the green eyes that shone with wetness. Why couldn't she be as beautiful as her sisters?

She reached for the small newspaper sticking out from under her table where she'd hidden it. She'd heard other girls talking about men needing brides over in the Americas, in the west where the land was still unsettled and everyone worked hard together to make a new start.

She needed a new start.

So she'd secretly asked one of the servants to pick her up a copy of a newspaper she'd heard was advertising for brides. Until now, she'd been too afraid to even look, sure she'd never have the courage to head to a new country on her own.

But in her heart, she knew it was the answer she was searching for.

All she had to do was find someone who she believed would treat her well and who could accept her as she was.

As she started to read through the advertisements, she knew she'd found her chance for a fresh start of her own.

CHAPTER 2

"You're making wagers you better intend to pay on." Brooks Vaughn stared across the table at the man who had sweat dripping from his forehead as he looked down at the cards in his hand. The man swallowed, his throat moving up and down rapidly.

"Oh, I'm good for it. You just better make sure ye know what ye're doing."

Brooks almost laughed out loud at the shakiness of Milton Hayward's voice as he tried to bluff. He'd played enough hands of poker to know that Milton was about to lose.

Milton was a regular in the saloon they were sitting in and Brooks knew he likely didn't have the money to cover the wager he was laying down.

But Brooks didn't care.

He'd come here to make a name for himself and winning was what he needed to do.

Brooks had spent too many years playing the game, waiting for the chance to go up against another man, a man who'd cheated his father, eventually costing him his life. If he had to spend every day sitting in the saloons playing against lowlifes like Milton Hayward, he was willing to do just that.

All Brooks knew about the man who'd cheated his father was his given name—Virgil. He was a gambler who moved from town to town, cheating and winning from hard-working folk who were down on their luck, hoping for a better chance.

He also knew the man had a scar that stretched from the top of one eye, down his cheek to the corner of his lips. Brooks had heard it was from a run-in with another man who hadn't taken kindly to being cheated.

The other man had been killed but Virgil carried the scar that Brooks had spent years waiting to see sitting across the table from him.

Laying his cards on the table, he kept his eyes on Milton taking note of the exact moment the man realized he'd lost. Even though Brooks had spent years learning the craft of gambling and he still despised it, he had to admit to feeling a small rush of excitement every time he won.

He avoided playing against ordinary people who were hoping for a big win to help pay debts or feed their families. Taking money from men who weren't as practiced as he was would make him no better than the man who'd done the same to his father.

So Brooks only sought out the seedier characters to play against, the ones who spent their days cheating regular men from their hard-earned money.

Milton was one of those men. He could be found sitting at these tables any day or night of the week and he was well known to be a swindler who'd think nothing of placing wagers that would cost many men their entire livelihood.

But Milton was also not a smart player. Everything he won, he'd lose just as fast, unable to turn down another wager with other men who were better than him.

"Let's see your hand."

He waited for Milton to lay his cards on the table.

"There's no way ye coulda beat me," Milton hissed.

Brooks lifted an eyebrow and glared at the man. "Are you accusing me of cheating?" His voice was low but it carried a threat along with the question. Around here, if you were calling another man a cheater, you'd better have the proof to back it up.

Milton threw his cards on the table, scattering them among the money and other cards already lying down.

Brooks stood, ready for a confrontation just as Milton pushed his own chair back.

"I ain't accusin' ye of nothin'. But I'll be keepin' a closer eye on ye the next time I sit at a table with you. That's a promise."

The two of them stood glaring at each other, both with their hands placed on the edge of the table, daring the other to move.

"Is there a problem here, boys?" The sound of his friend's voice broke through Brooks' anger. He stood up straight and turned to face the town sheriff who'd just walked over.

"No problem at all, Lewis. Simply settling up the wager Milton here just lost. Isn't that right, Milton?" He turned back and smiled at the man who was still standing with his fists tightly at his sides, glaring at Brooks.

"That's right. No problems here, Sheriff." The words came out through clenched teeth.

"It's time to pay up, Milton. You made a fairly hefty bet on that last hand, so I hope you have the money to cover it." He was enjoying watching Milton scramble to come up with a way to pay his debt, the same way Milton had done to others.

Milton glanced at the sheriff who was still standing and watching the exchange, before bringing his eyes back to Brooks.

"I don't reckon I have the full amount at the moment. But I'm willin' to put somethin' else up until I can get the money to pay you." The man who'd always been willing to take anything he could get from others was now trying to find something he could use to pay Brooks.

Brooks loved watching him squirm.

"What if I'm not prepared to take your deal? What could you possibly have to offer that'd be worth what you're owing me?"

A sneer spread across Milton's face that made the hair on the back of Brooks' neck stand up. "Oh, I got something you'd like. I know you've got that sister of yers holed up out on your farm and it must be a worry when ye're in town playing cards."

Brooks strode over closer to Milton, uneasy with the direction he was going with his offer. "Leave my sister out of this." They lived alone and he was the only family she had left to help care for her.

Milton put his hands up in front of him as Brooks got near. "Whoa! I'm not suggestin' anything bad. In fact, what I've got to offer just might be something ye could use for her needs, as well as yer own."

The man wasn't making any sense at all.

"What are you offering, Milton? I don't have all day to stand here listening to you ramble."

Just then the door to the saloon opened and light spread into the room. Brooks shielded his eyes which had become accustomed to the darkness.

He could make out the silhouette of what looked like a woman holding a bag. As his eyes adjusted, he saw her standing there in a long dress, with a bonnet covering her head. Her head scanned the crowd along the long bar, her eyes flickering away in obvious embarrassment at the imitation nude masterpieces of the Renaissance painters about the room. She looked respectable, not a shady woman or a saloon girl, and he had to admire her courage to walk into a seedy establishment like this on her own.

Milton gave a little laugh as he nodded his head in the direction of the door. "That's what I'm offerin'. A woman, just for you."

AVAILABLE NOW

ABOUT THE AUTHOR

USA Today Bestselling Author Kay P. Dawson writes sweet western romance – the kind that leaves out all of the juicy details and immerses you in a true, heartfelt love story. Growing up pretending she was Laura Ingalls, she's always had a love for the old west and pioneer times. She believes in true love, and finding your happy ever after.

Happily married mom of two girls, Kay has always taught her children to follow their dreams. And, after a breast cancer diagnosis at the age of 39, she realized it was time to take her own advice. She had always wanted to write a book, and she decided that the someday she was waiting for was now.

She writes western historical, contemporary and time travel romance that all transport the reader to a time or place where true love always finds a way.